"I advise you to save your moonshine for those who would appreciate it."

It occurred to her now that he would make an unforgiving enemy. Before she could do or say anything further he had reached out, drawing her toward him.

"I have a mind to tumble you from the heights of your arrogance, my fair beauty. I could so easily humble you."

He pulled her against him in a viselike grip. She could feel his strength against her, making her seem weak by comparison. His lips claimed hers in a cruel and seeking kiss. Her heart had begun beating fast from the moment his hand had touched her flesh, but the effect of his lips upon hers was like that of a flint spark on tinder, turning her blood into molten metal, gushing through her veins and igniting her entire soul in a conflagration that threatened to consume her entirely....

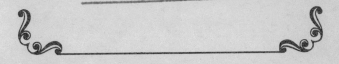

Also by Rachelle Edwards
Published by Fawcett Books:

THE
DEVILISH
EARL

Rachelle Edwards

FAWCETT CREST • NEW YORK

A Fawcett Crest Book
Published by Ballantine Books
Copyright © 1994 by Rachelle Edwards

Library of Congress Catalog Card Number: 94-94425

ISBN 0-449-22321-3

Manufactured in the United States of America

First Edition: October 1994

10 9 8 7 6 5 4 3 2 1

ONE

"Alas, alack, I am undone! This is the end of me. I am betrayed by a faithless swain. My life has been for naught, and it is better it should end so I suffer this purgatory no longer. Good-bye, Papa. Good-bye, my friends. I die and shall be no more."

The small figure on the stage, clad in a simple white muslin gown, fell back onto the daybed, uttered a heartrending sigh, and was still. The other actors on the stage bowed their heads in unspoken grief.

In the sparsely occupied auditorium there was an unusual hush, even in the normally noisy and often abusive pit, for the few seconds it took for the curtains to be closed on the tragic scene. Then, amid the clearly discernible sobs of those affected by the tragedy enacted before them, applause broke out, gaining momentum as the actors appeared before the curtain to receive their acclaim.

The actress who had expired with such pathos and reality a few moments earlier now bounced back to life, beaming at the applause she was receiving while curtsying to all parts of the auditorium.

"Bravo!" a lone voice called out from the gallery, and the actress looked up to bestow on the unseen

1

admirer a dazzling smile that lit up her entire countenance.

A slight figure in her filmy muslin gown, she continued to accept her due before filing off the stage with the others at last.

Sir Hubert Patch, who had been enjoying the drama from the box closest to the stage, along with some of his cronies, dabbed away a tear with a lawn handkerchief.

"By all that's blue, Hu!" Lord Silverwood scoffed as he allowed his quizzing glass to drop. "You cannot be affected by such humbug."

"You have no soul, my friend," Sir Hubert replied, his voice still thick with emotion. "Only one immured from true feeling could be scathing of such fine melodrama, and so profound a performance."

Lord Silverwood laughed in acknowledgment of the truth of that statement as Captain Fielding declared, "It is an admitted fact that Blaise Silverwood cannot in any circumstances be moved by female histrionics."

"I'll have you know, Johnny, that faculty has stood me in very good stead for many years," the earl laughingly replied as he got to his feet.

"Then it is all the more surprising you have a fancy for actresses," Sir Hubert mused.

"*Actresses*, not acting."

"Do they know when to stop acting?" Sir Hubert inquired. "Forgive the question, Sil, but as you are an acknowledged expert on actresses, I can think of no one more able to answer my question."

"In the boudoir, I may remind you, it scarce matters," Lord Silverwood responded, a wry look on his handsome face.

When the three gentlemen began to make their

2

way out of the shabby theater, they exacted curious and admiring glances as they went. For the local townspeople the presence of such obvious Corinthians was a novelty. Few had ever before clapped eyes upon such exquisitely turned-out gentlemen of quality. However, those who were conversant with such matters would recognize that only Lord Silverwood could be deigned a nonpareil; the others were mere dandies.

While the three gentlemen waited for their carriage to arrive, Lord Silverwood paused to glance at the playbill of *The Betrayed Wife*, the excruciating melodrama he had just endured. The heroine, however, *had* taken his attention, even though he had feigned indifference to his friends. Despite the appalling dialogue and hammy acting, she stood out, both for her youth and beauty and a genuine talent that in this instance was given little chance to shine; but he had no intention of revealing his opinion of her to his companions.

Stacia Gilbert, he mused, repeating her name to himself thoughtfully. Although he was resident in the area for only a short time, he wondered if closer acquaintance with Miss Gilbert might be rewarding. It would certainly serve to relieve his habitual boredom. Despite his wealth, good looks, and popularity, and although he participated in all the diversions open to a prominent member of the beau monde, Blaise de Courcy, Earl of Silverwood, was finding life increasingly tedious of late. He had no notion why it was so, but there was little remedy he could so far discover beyond the purely fleeting.

"I don't believe Hu would have been so affected by the play," Captain Fielding mused, "if the heroine hadn't been so fetching."

Lord Silverwood smiled sardonically in the darkness as Sir Hubert replied, "Well, naturally not. As an actress she ain't in the class of Sarah Siddons or *La* Jordan, but she is a fetching bit of muslin, which is bound to affect her reception by an audience. I did note that some of the ladies in the audience were similarly affected by the melodrama. Stacia Gilbert, eh? Might send the chit a posy. What do you say, Sil?"

"I say she has probably never seen the like of Sir Hubert Patch in all her born days."

"Now, you're roasting me," Sir Hubert replied in a sulky tone. "I don't possess your looks and address, Sil, so don't blame me for trying for a green girl. I haven't your way with words."

"Who has?" Captain Fielding asked with heavy irony. "What did you really think of the chit, Silverwood?"

"She was distinctly more fetching than Mrs. . . ."

As he searched for the name, Captain Fielding supplied, "Sanbourne. Marietta Sanbourne, the leading actress. Overlaced mutton, more like. Miss Gilbert has a definite edge, even if it is only in her youth."

"Oh, indeed," Sir Hubert agreed. "In any event I'm persuaded actresses are finished by the time they reach one and twenty."

"They are if they ally themselves to Silverwood." Captain Fielding chuckled.

"I've a mind to call you out for that unjust accusation," the earl responded.

"That wasn't meant to be an insult, Blaise, and where would you find seconds in Dorrington, I wonder?"

"I shall be obliged to beat you at whist instead."

4

"If that is the choice before me, I'd liefer have pistols at dawn! I'd be less out-of-pocket."

His friend laughed as Sir Hubert mused, "The ladies of the Gala Troupe could possibly serve to brighten a wet weekend in the Midlands. There's more than one fetching female in the company, I noticed."

"What would be the use of asking?" Captain Fielding asked, wrinkling his nose derisively. "When they clap eyes upon Silverwood, even when he shows a marked disinterest in *them*, it is bound to result in a lonely weekend for you and me, Hu."

"You're beside the bridle on this one, Johnny," Sir Hubert replied. "Blaise Silverwood has never been interested in green girls or overlaced mutton, so we run a sporting chance. Is that not so?"

The earl reached into his pocket and drew out his snuffbox, taking a pinch with just his thumb and forefinger. As he replaced the gold box into his pocket, he replied thoughtfully, "Miss Gilbert did not appear so green to me, Hu. You mustn't compare females who take to the boards in quite the same light as our sisters, who stay in the schoolroom until they come out. An actress of sixteen or so is often less green than our sisters at five and twenty. The chit has probably enjoyed more than the one gallant by now."

"What a pity the role didn't call for her to wear breeches," Sir Hubert mused as the earl eyed him with amusement. "I rather like to see a female in breeches, and where else is it possible than on the stage?"

"Where is the carriage?" Captain Fielding muttered, glancing around the almost deserted street now that the small theater crowd had dispersed into nearby inns and taverns. "I'm beginning to feel a mite sharp-set and look forward to my supper."

Just at that moment the carriage swerved around the corner and Lord Silverwood stepped back, saying hastily, "Go along without me, gentlemen. I shall join you presently."

Sir Hubert gasped. "By gad, you have taken color with the chit, have you not?" When the earl forebore to reply, his friend added slyly, "Or is it the old cat, perchance, who draws you back?"

When Lord Silverwood still refused to reply but merely smiled maddeningly, Captain Fielding murmured, "If the wind's in that direction, better you and I content ourselves with a game of backgammon, Hu!"

Stacia Gilbert felt totally breathless as she came off the stage, the crowd's acclaim still ringing in her ears. "Did you hear that applause?" she gasped. "I declare I have never heard the like before."

Her dark eyes were wide and luminous, and her pale cheeks, with white powder still clinging to them from the death scene, were unusually pink.

"Do not delude yourself it was entirely for you, child," Marietta Sanbourne warned, "for I assure you it was not. That last scene was vastly overacted."

"The audience was in tears," Maura Copeland, one of the other members of the troupe, protested, glancing at Stacia's crestfallen face. "One gentleman swooned away and was carried out by his companions, and as it was during Stacia's death scene, you cannot quarrel with *that*."

"There is acting and *over*acting, as I have often stated," Mrs. Sanbourne persisted.

"Then you evidently subscribe to the latter school of thought!" Maura responded.

Marietta Sanbourne threw back her head in a haughty manner. "For one who does not even know what the most basic form of acting involves, I take that comment amiss, madam!"

"You can take it how you like, Mrs. Sanbourne, but the truth is, the audience loved Stacia's performance tonight."

"The audience," Mrs. Sanbourne scoffed. "The audience! I wonder you can consider them such. Chawbacons to a man."

"They pay to come in, nevertheless," Maura persisted.

"Ladies! Ladies! Enough of this brangling," a voice boomed from the wings.

"Ormerod!" Mrs. Sanbourne cried. "Am I obliged to suffer this Turkish treatment from *minor* members of the troupe?"

"No pulling caps, ladies, I shall not allow it in my company," Ormerod Greaves, the actor/manager of the Gala Troupe, warned. "Suffice the takings at the box office during this engagement have ensured we shall *eat* next week. I'm persuaded you will all agree with me that is a matter for great rejoicing."

"That is indeed wonderful news," Stacia responded, her pleasure undimmed by Mrs. Sanbourne's criticism of her shining moment.

"I wish you would be kind enough to instruct the owner of this miserable establishment to trim the wicks of his lamps," Mrs. Sanbourne told him. "They flicker abominably and hurt my eyes."

She then swept into her dressing room and closed the door before Ormerod Greaves had a chance to reply. "Marietta," he called after her, but he was faced with a closed dressing-room door. "Oh, dear, she is in a pucker," he lamented.

"When is she not?" Maura Copeland asked, and several other members of the company murmured their agreement.

"I will not have Mrs. Sanbourne cut up in this manner," Ormerod Greaves told them. "She is simply divine, and I expect you all to hold her in the highest esteem."

"One cannot hold her in as high esteem as she does herself," one actor called out.

"Oh, do go to your dressing rooms," Mr. Greaves told them irritably before beaming at Stacia. "Your performance was commendable, my dear," he told her, and her gamine features broke into a smile again, "but do not, I entreat you, let Mrs. Sanbourne know I told you so. I don't wish to break straws with her."

"They truly enjoyed my acting, Mr. Greaves?"

"Yes, my dear, they certainly did."

Both Stacia and Maura went into their shared dressing room, and each of them shivered in turn.

"How I wish we had comfortable dressing rooms," Stacia said in heartfelt tones, "or am I asking for too much?"

"You're asking for the impossible," was her companion's reply. "All these theaters are miserable slums, and none of Marietta Sanbourne's affectations can change that. We ought to be used to it, although"—she turned to Stacia—"I have the feeling you might be bound for better things." Stacia looked at her curiously. "Of late you have been received so warmly. No wonder Mrs. Sanbourne is jaundiced toward you. I regard her as smoky."

"You really mustn't say so, Maura. Mrs. Sanbourne is a fine actress who has taught me much."

"It's a relief she hasn't taught you her 'nerves.'" Stacia laughed, and Maura went on with more seriousness. "Mark my words—you will have a brilliant future. I'll wager by the time you are half Mrs. Sanbourne's age, you will be at Covent Garden or Drury Lane."

For a moment Stacia was taken aback, and then she laughed. "What a funster you are!"

"On this occasion I am serious, I assure you."

A flicker of consternation crossed Stacia's face as she responded, "Then your attic's to let, Maura. Covent Garden or Drury Lane indeed!"

"I'll warrant their dressing rooms are not cold or drafty. You ought to think to the future, Stacia. You surely must be aware by now that you don't have to stay touring the provinces for the rest of your life."

Stacia's ebullience, which had been unquenchable since the end of the evening's performance, was suddenly sobered. "I don't ever think of the future, only the present, and I like being with this company, even when we do perform in drafty booths at country fairs. It's hardly worse than here, is it?"

Maura Copeland looked at Stacia consideringly before she ventured, "But you're not really like us, Stacia. You're Quality."

Stacia had been attempting to clean off her makeup in the cracked and spotted mirror. "I'm just like you!" she protested rather heatedly.

Maura turned away. "Did you see those young gentlemen in the box tonight?"

"No . . ."

"Quality, they were. No doubt about it." Involun-

9

tarily Stacia shivered, telling herself it was the draft that caused her to do so. "They were top of the trees, and each one of them couldn't keep his eyes off you, Stacia. Wouldn't it be wonderful if one of them was the manager of one of the London patent theaters?"

Stacia laughed uneasily, and as she did so, someone tapped on the door. Maura went to open it to find the callboy standing in the corridor. "A basket of flowers for Miss Gilbert," he announced.

"There! I told you so!" Maura cried, taking them in.

Stacia laughed more easily now. "Flowers? For me?"

"Aren't you going to read the card?" Maura asked, and she looked as excited as she would had the flowers been for her.

Rather reluctantly Stacia took it, her hand trembling slightly. The missive was addressed to Atalanta, her character in the play, and the card read, *"Join me for supper, fair Atalanta, so I may have the opportunity of bringing you back to life and restoring your faith in mankind."*

It was written in a bold, flowing script and signed *Silverwood.* Stacia gasped as she took in the aristocratic crest on the card, which fluttered from her fingers as if it had suddenly caught fire. Looking puzzled, Maura retrieved it from the dusty floor. After she had read it, she let out a cry of triumph.

"Well done! If you play a good hand, I shouldn't wonder if you'll earn yourself a grand villa in Hampstead Village one day soon."

Stacia pulled her shawl about her. "I have no intention of going to supper with him."

Maura Copeland looked astounded. "Not . . . going! Now I know your attic's to let. Do you regard old Finnigan's supper so appetizing, you can pass up this offer?"

Stacia thought of their landlord's usual fare of stringy fowl and fatty meat and continued to look grim.

"You are funning. Tell me you're bamming me, Stacia."

"Indeed, I am not. I would need to be starving before I break bread with some lecherous old goat like Lord Silverwood."

"Old? Who says he is old? Have you taken leave of your senses, girl?" When Maura received no reply, she cried, "Would that I could go in your stead."

Suddenly Stacia became animated. She thrust the basket back at the callboy, who had been listening wide-eyed. "There has been some mistake, Billy. These were meant for Mrs. Sanbourne. Take them to her dressing room, if you please."

"No!" Maura cried as Stacia began to close the door on the callboy. "The flowers were meant for *you*. Atalanta was your name in the play."

"Mrs. Sanbourne will not notice in her eagerness to take supper with Lord Silverwood. She is the most awful snob and couldn't possibly conceive he would want to solicit my company."

"I don't understand your attitude."

"It doesn't matter, Maura. Please unhook my gown. I've lingered here long enough, and I've a mind to be away to our lodging before either of us contracts a chill."

"Ha!" Maura exclaimed as she obliged. "You're right to be in a fidge to return to such a palace. 'Tis no wonder you begrudge every moment you spend away from it. You're only fit for Bedlam—you know

11

that, don't you? Lord Silverwood will be taking Mrs. Sanbourne for supper while you feast on pig swill!"

Looking grim, Stacia replied as she stepped out of her stage gown, "Good. They deserve each other."

"How could you possibly know?"

Stacia didn't answer. She just turned to unhook Maura's gown. "Mrs. Sanbourne won't be such a chucklehead," Maura warned her.

"I don't doubt she will bask in his attention. It won't worry her that Lord Silverwood probably has a wife in a grand house in Mayfair."

Maura looked at her in astonishment. "What has that to do with anything, I ask you? A *chère amie* can live in as much comfort in Bloomsbury or Hampstead as a wife in Mayfair. Just consider Mrs. Jordan or Mrs. Clarke. They have royal princes as their *chèrs amis*. Prinny's granted Mrs. Robinson a pension to keep her warm since the end of their relationship."

Stacia laughed without mirth. "Now, if one of the princes were to ask me, I might be in a different frame of mind."

"Nasty, fat gentlemen, they are."

"Mayhap so is Lord Silverwood. We cannot possibly know."

"You might as well enter a nunnery here and now if that is to be your attitude toward admirers."

"Don't think I haven't considered it," she replied as Maura fastened her gown.

"Our best hope is to find some wealthy protector." Stacia shuddered and put on her hat as Maura added, "You're an enigma, Stacia Gilbert, that's what you are."

"I'd liefer be an enigma than a lightskirt."

"Pride and propriety won't keep you warm on a cold winter's night, nor fill an empty stomach with food."

When they were dressed and ready to go, Marietta Sanbourne came rushing out of her dressing room. "I'm taking supper with Lord Silverwood," she cried, and Maura Copeland drew in a sharp breath while casting a glance at Stacia, whose cheeks had become quite pink. "The *Earl* of Silverwood!" Mrs. Sanbourne added for good measure.

"How very nice for you, ma'am," Stacia told her in an even voice.

"To be entertained by those of an elevated situation is a perk for those of us who are truly talented, my dear."

As she hurried away, Maura said through clenched teeth, "It is not to be borne. Do you truly not wish to be in her place this evening?"

Suddenly Stacia relaxed and began to laugh. "No! Not for anything. But I would give a great deal to see Lord Silverwood's face when Marietta Sanbourne climbs into his carriage!"

TWO

Stacia remained awake long after the lodging house had fallen silent. She had heard a carriage clatter to a standstill on the cobbles outside and listened to Marietta Sanbourne's shrill laughter moments afterward. On the other side of the bed, Maura snored gently, sighing from time to time.

For once the clammy chill of the unheated room and unaired sheets did not pervade her consciousness. She had grown used to the frequently hard life of a strolling actress after the comfort of her early childhood, but there were often times when she ached to enjoy the luxury she had once known.

There were often weeks when the receipts could not provide enough food to satisfy their hunger, and Stacia couldn't recall when last she had purchased a new gown. Her sewing skills ensured a neatly darned garment, but she never dwelled upon how shabby she must look. Despite all the drawbacks of the life, she knew full well she was one of the fortunates, for she had witnessed far worse hardship for others along the way.

Just now her mind seethed with thoughts far removed from her own discomfort, now that a reminder of the past had been thrust upon her so unexpectedly.

Silverwood. How odd that name should return to

haunt her after all these years. It was a name she
had resolutely consigned to the very depths of her
consciousness, where she had hoped it would stay
forever, but now the memories came flooding back,
and she found she could recall it all too clearly despite the passage of time.

She remembered sitting on the stairs at Dover's
End, the beautiful Tudor manor house that had
been in her family for almost three hundred years.

Eustacia Farramond, eight years old, sat on the
cold stair, listening to her father's raised voice in
the study below. As she listened, she clutched her
rag doll close to her for the comfort she could not
find elsewhere. After she had been sitting there for
some considerable time, she had become afraid, for
her father's voice became angrier and the stranger's almost equal to it.

A sound on the stair behind her made her look
up to see her elder brother, Damian, summoned
home from Eton on a matter of urgency she did not
yet understand.

"Eustacia, what are you doing here?"

His voice bore an edge of irritation she didn't
fully understand either, although she had been
aware of a certain atmosphere in the house of late,
a whispering among the servants that ceased
whenever she came near.

"Papa has a visitor from London, not a welcome
one, from all I observe."

"You observe too much for a child."

"I am not a child!" she protested. "I shall be nine
next birthday. Who is the visitor?"

"I don't know."

"Papa sounds exceedingly angry. Do you think he
will challenge the man to a duel?"

Damian sighed and sat down on the stair beside her. "No. It's nothing like that."

"Papa's been angry of late, Damian. He rang a peal over me yesterday for nothing at all."

"He has had weighty matters on his mind, Eustacia. He's been gambling again."

"All gentlemen gamble," she replied, with a wisdom way beyond her years.

"Yes, but this time Papa's really dished himself. He can't raise the wind any longer. He's run off his legs, at *point nonplus*."

Stacia frowned at hearing the young man's jargon. "What does that mean, Damian?"

The young man looked uncompromisingly grim. "If I am not mistaken, we're without a rag. Put in the simplest terms, my dear sweet sister, you won't be able to buy all those pretty little gewgaws you're so fond of whenever you go into Buckham with Miss Tiplady. In fact," he added darkly, "it's probable we won't be able to retain Miss Tiplady herself for very much longer."

Stacia was just frowning and trying to understand what her brother was saying to her when the study door flew open, attracting her attention once again.

"So there's an end to it!" her father cried, his cheeks ruddy. "You may go to the devil, sir!"

"You cannot apportion blame to me for this imbroglio, sir," the other man insisted.

"No, no. I have brought this ruination on myself. To be brought to buckle and thong is a calamity I cannot yet comprehend, but no doubt I will when I am obliged to explain it to my poor motherless children. Much you care!"

As he swayed slightly on his feet, his daughter

stood up, but Damian put out one hand to stay her. The visitor accepted his hat, gloves, and cane from the butler, and as he did so, he suddenly became aware of the two young people on the stairs. He turned to look at them, but his gaze seemed to rest solely on Eustacia.

To her child's mind he appeared to be no older than Damian, although she knew some boys gambled just as feverishly as their elders. His boyish appearance was belied by his height and the breadth of his shoulders. Mere youth that he was, he bore no likeness to the young men of the area to whom she was more accustomed. There was a stylishness about him the child found fascinating as well as alien.

His hair was very dark and curled into a fashionable disarray. His eyes were so dark, they appeared to be black, and when they raked over her, Eustacia began to tremble with fear. She shrank back against the banister rail as if that futile gesture would save her from his merciless scrutiny.

His glance lasted only the few moments before he left, but it seemed to be an eternity to the frightened child. To her, in the flickering lamplight there was something quite diabolical about him, and she knew instinctively, without her brother's hints echoing in her ears, that this young man boded ill for her and for her family.

The door closed, and the subsequent clatter of carriage wheels indicated his departure. Eustacia continued to stare at the closed door, the rag doll clutched protectively to her heart.

Devin Farramond transferred his despairing look to his children. Then he straightened up and said,

"Damian, Eustacia, I should like words with you in the study, if you please."

Eustacia exchanged a fearful look with her brother before they both filed silently into the study, where their father was pouring himself a large measure of brandy. From the unsteadiness of his gait, the glass, brimful of alcohol, was by no means his first.

"A calamity has come upon us," he pronounced the moment he had downed the amber liquid. "The enormity of it you can scarce comprehend."

"Papa . . . ?" Eustacia began. "Who was that man?"

"Don't interrupt me, child. This is difficult enough for me without contending with that also." He kept his eyes studiously averted from either of his children as he went on, "There is no simple way for me to tell you—we're all dished up. Lord Silverwood cannot see his way to waiting any longer for his dues."

"Was it hazard?" Damian asked, by no means surprised by his father's disclosure. Devin Farramond nodded. "Lord Silverwood," the boy spat out contemptuously. "You were probably foxed when he fleeced you of your property."

"Silence, boy! Don't be so impudent or I'll take my cane to your rump, sir!" When Eustacia began to sob, Mr. Farramond looked shamefaced. "Aye," he admitted, "he's a devil, all right. A true devil."

"Everyone knows his reputation. He's a hellrake and a reckless gamester." There was a brief silence before Damian asked, "Shall I be able to return to Eton next term?"

"Your grandpapa provided for your education, Damian. There is no problem with that, but we shall be obliged to vacate the house. It must be sold to raise the wind." Both children gasped. "Your uncle Quentin has offered us a home at Brackentree."

"Uncle Quentin!" Damian cried. "Oh, no! I'd as lief be thrown on the parish as be obliged to live as a basket scrambler on Uncle Quentin's charity."

"Silence, boy! I'll not have you cut up your uncle in that fashion."

"You call him a clutchfist yourself. How could you do this to us, Papa?"

Devin Farramond looked totally stricken, and Eustacia whirled round on her brother. "You mustn't blame Papa. It is Lord Silverwood's fault entirely we're in the suds. He must be a totally odious man to turn us to bag and wallet!"

"It is Papa who is the gamester. His lordship is only taking what is his." He looked to his father again, and there was unusual passion in his manner as he added, "You have ruined my life, sir! I shall never forgive you for it!"

So saying, he turned on his heel and rushed out of the room.

"Damian!" Mr. Farramond cried. "Damian, don't go!" He swayed back on his heels once again before he sank down onto his chair.

"Papa, are you ill?" Eustacia asked as a new concern afflicted her.

Mr. Farramond pulled at his neck cloth while waving with one hand toward the decanter. "Just a little brandy, child. Your brother for all his youth is too high in the instep for my liking. Takes after his mother's family, I daresay."

Eustacia's small hand shook as she filled a glass to the brim with brandy. "Damian won't remain in the dismals for long," she told him as she watched

19

anxiously while he downed it, and then to her relief his color returned.

"Wouldn't blame him if he does. This is a bad business, Eustacia. It's not what I wanted for us all—to be under the hatches and at the mercy of that nip-cheese brother of mine—but there is no alternative that I can find." He buried his face in his hands. "I've betrayed you and your brother, and I know it, but this reverse in our fortunes is only an interlude. We'll come about, child. Indeed we will."

As he reached for the decanter, he added, "You'll have a Season in London when you're old enough and a press full of gowns in all the latest styles." He reached out to pat her hand. "You'll be all the crack, my dear. Just you see if you won't."

The eight-year-old child bit her lip while her father devoured another glass of brandy as if his life depended upon it.

From what little she knew of her uncle Quentin and aunt Tess, she was filled with trepidation for what the future was about to hold.

THREE

Marietta Sanbourne stood in the wings, observing Stacia singing a sweet and plaintive song during the burletta that followed a well-received melodrama. Earlier Stacia had also made a solemn audience roar with laughter during the farce.

Ormerod Greaves joined his leading lady, and Marietta linked her arm into his. "She sings quite prettily," the actress owned.

"She is at last learning to project herself and her voice," the actor agreed, his booming voice little suited to the whisper he was now obliged to affect.

"It has taken her long enough, in all conscience," Mrs. Sanbourne replied. "She has been with us for several years and for most of it suited to nothing better than prompting and dressing."

"We all need to serve our apprenticeship, Marietta," he reminded her.

"Not I, Ormerod. The talent was born in me, as you well know. Miss Gilbert is a trifler. She is biding her time. Life as an actress does not sit on her well. Her background, whatever it may be, makes her unsuited."

"Do I detect a little envy in your tone, madam?"

The woman bridled. "Indeed you do not. How unjust you are to level that accusation at me. A green girl! La! I hope I do not see the day when such a creature makes Marietta Sanbourne smoky!" Mr. Greaves cast her an amused glance as the actress went on, "Miss Gilbert is still fit only to be an ingenue. Let us see her tackle roles like Lady Macbeth or Desdemona. Then we shall see her true mettle!"

"She will do so in due course. Let us hope that when she does speak the lines of the immortal Bard, Marietta, she does not elicit the laughter you did in Manchester."

"The audience were peasants. Peasants," she spat out. "I recall that you were equally dismissive when one of them declared you were the ham in Hamlet."

Mr. Greaves's face became dark as he replied, "You've touched me on the raw there, m'dear, but let us cry pax before we resort to parting brass rags."

Marietta Sanbourne smiled at him indulgently. "My dear Ormerod, if we have not contrived to do so in all our long years of acquaintanceship, we shall not do so now."

"In any event, Miss Gilbert's fame has spread swiftly," Mr. Greaves told her, now scarcely able to conceal his glee. "Almost a full house this evening, and that bodes well for all of us, my dear."

Marietta Sanbourne drew herself up to full height. "I'll grant the chit one thing: she has had the privilege of observing a great actress at work since she joined us. That must have served her well."

"Oh, indeed," he agreed, but all the while he didn't take his attention from Stacia.

"Quite a little mystery, our little Miss Gilbert," Mrs. Sanbourne mused.

"None of us has a past worth talking about, although I own Miss Gilbert has a touch of the Quality about her."

Marietta Sanbourne sniffed derisively. "Shabby genteel, more like."

"Talking of Quality," Ormerod Greaves murmured, studiously keeping his attention on Stacia, "I hear you were given supper by a nonpareil."

At the mention of her achievement the woman dimpled at last. "Everyone must be talking about my good fortune."

"You should first ascertain his lordship's intentions before you cry roast meat, my dear."

"Lord Silverwood is a gentleman through and through, Ormerod."

The actor turned at last to look at her. "What did he say to you? What did he promise?"

Mrs. Sanbourne looked maddeningly coy. "Oh, my dear, you mustn't press me on that score, for the memory of the evening I spent in his company is far too precious for me to tell."

Ormerod Greaves looked irritated and said, "You really are a silly goose, Marietta. I cannot conceive why I hold you in such high regard when you persist in acting like a chucklehead."

Just at that moment Stacia came bounding off the stage to yet more resounding applause. There were times in the past when she'd been unable to tell for whom the applause was intended, if for anyone in particular. Of late, however, there was no mistaking her own popularity with the audience, and their applause was heady.

"You are doing tolerably well, my dear," Mrs. Sanbourne informed her, making no effort to hide her patronizing manner. "In a few years' time it is possible you might have become quite good."

"Thank you, ma'am," Stacia replied in all humility, but she had become fully aware that it was the paying patrons who decided who was good and not Marietta Sanbourne.

"You have learned well, but you have had the advantage of observing me for a number of years, which is bound to have assisted you."

Stacia grinned. "Indeed, ma'am. When I joined the company, it's true I knew nothing."

Mrs. Sanbourne appeared mollified, casting Ormerod Greaves a triumphant look, and then, just as Stacia was about to go past her, she hesitated to inquire in the most innocent of tones, "Mrs. Sanbourne, did you enjoy your supper with Lord Silverwood? Everyone is agog to know."

The older woman looked almost smug as she replied, "It was most enjoyable."

"Will . . . will you be meeting again, do you think?"

"I have no doubt of it." She turned to look out into the auditorium. "He's been here again this evening, on his own this time. I saw him watching me from his box. He scarce took his eyes from me all the while I was onstage."

Stacia's own smile faded somewhat as she followed the woman's gaze, but all she could see was a glimpse of his back as he was leaving.

"Mrs. Sanbourne has been boasting to all who will listen," Maura confided when Stacia joined her in the dressing room. "No wonder she didn't mind that you've roundly upstaged her in *The Betrayed Wife*."

"I didn't mean to," Stacia told her truthfully.

"You couldn't help it, you silly goose. You have youth and talent. She has neither."

"You're being a mite unfair, Maura. Mrs. Sanbourne has her following." Then Stacia said more briskly, "Maura, let us change and go for supper as soon as we are able. I've no mind to delay and perhaps contract a chill in this drafty barn."

"I wonder what our next venue will be like?"

"Salisbury." Stacia frowned. "This will be my first appearance at the theater, but it's far enough away, I fancy."

Maura paused to glance at her as she folded up Stacia's costume. "Far enough away from where?"

Stacia hesitated for a moment before she retorted, "From here, I suppose."

"The scene of your triumph," Maura mocked.

"One town is much like another. You must have noticed the grim lodgings, drafty theaters with their hoop-lights that make your eyes sore."

"I can't gainsay you on that, Stacia. Here, let me unhook your gown and we can be gone from here before anyone else has the temerity to send you flowers. That would be outside of enough!"

Stacia's cheeks grew pink. As an actress, although she had never thought highly of her own talents, she had hoped her thoughts would not be quite so transparent.

As Maura hurriedly dressed to guard against the cold that permeated every part of the old theater, Stacia hesitated, glancing critically at her reflection in the cracked and spotted pier glass.

There was no likeness she could detect to that eight-year-old child who had waited fearfully on the stairs, the one who had felt Lord Silverwood's stare would draw out her very soul. The memory of that night was as fresh as if it had happened only yesterday. In the dark recesses of her mind, she

25

had been afraid since first setting eyes on the note that somehow he knew who she was and had come to mock her, but he couldn't possibly recognize Stacia Gilbert from the young Eustacia Farramond.

As she stared at her murky reflection, she was aware that, despite the intervening years, the same pair of wide, frightened eyes were staring back at her, waiflike in the light from the solitary, smelly lamp. She pulled off her wig and watched as her curls tumbled around her shoulders.

"Stacia, you'll catch your death, standing there in your shift."

Stacia transferred her attention to Maura, who was now fully dressed and almost ready to leave. For a long moment she stared at her unseeingly, recalling that from the very beginning of her association with the Gala Troupe, it had been Maura Copeland who had looked after her, taking her under her wing like a mother hen when other members tried to take advantage of her or put her down.

All at once Stacia smiled. "I cannot conceive why I'm troubling my head in this foolish manner."

"Nor I."

"I'm cork-brained, am I not?"

"Let us hope you don't attract too many beaux in the future, my dear, if this is the effect one gentleman's attentions have had upon you."

" 'Tis nothing of the sort," Stacia retorted as she reached for her gown. "It's simply that I have never played so many leading roles before and am overwhelmed by my reception."

"It would be better for the troupe if you played even more leading roles. Fresh young talent is always preferable to a Bartholomew Baby like Marietta Sanbourne! You have the additional advantage of being a better actress."

Her observations made Stacia laugh, something she had done little of since Lord Silverwood had intruded upon the life she had made for herself. His presence in Dorrington had somehow soured the success of her appearances onstage.

"Have you never relished playing leading roles?" Stacia asked her friend, all at once curious, for questions of any kind were rarely asked among members of the troupe.

"I know my limitations," Maura replied, looking rueful. "I play supporting roles well enough, and that provides me with a roof over my head and a meal in my stomach—usually." Stacia grinned knowingly, for there had been times, many of them, when they'd all gone to bed hungry. "I don't have the talent to be a leading player, nor the looks to attract a beau to protect me. You, my dear, could have both with very little effort, and I urge you to think on the matter carefully before your youth and beauty fade, which they do soon enough. You only have to observe Mrs. Sanbourne to acknowledge that sad fact."

Stacia's smile faded, but before she had any chance to formulate an answer, there came a knock at the door.

"La! It is just as I surmised." Maura chuckled. "More flowers from your faithful following, you mark my words."

As Maura went to open the door, Stacia froze with fear, totally oblivious to the fact that she stood there clad only in a linen shift, one that scarcely provided any covering at all.

"What have you got for us this time, Billy . . . ?"

27

Maura started to ask, but her voice died away and she stepped back when she saw the gentleman standing in the doorway.

"I considered it prudent to deliver this myself," the stranger replied, holding up a posy as he added ironically, "Billy seems prone to delivering to the wrong person."

In his black evening coat, set off to perfection by a pristine white shirt and crisp neck cloth tied *en cascade* with great precision, Lord Silverwood looked quite out of place in the dingy corridor outside their dressing room. He was carrying an exquisitely arranged posy of spring violets, which looked equally incongruous in his strong brown hand. Although he had not entered the room, he seemed to fill and dominate it.

Just as Stacia had become a woman since her first encounter with Lord Silverwood, the boy had become a man, a very handsome one, dashing some of Stacia's preconceptions about him. In the years that had passed since their first encounter, she had comforted herself with the possibility he had descended into a rakehell, but amazingly there was no sign of dissipation on his face, no slackness about the jaw or lips, and his eyes were clear and as probing as she recalled. If she had hoped to see a sad wreck, old beyond his years, bowed down by his own debauchery, she was bound for disappointment.

Maura hesitated for a moment, looking discomfited at her own dilemma before she sketched a brief curtsy to the earl and murmured, "I'll wait for you outside, Stacia dear."

Stacia seemed totally bereft of speech and therefore was unable to prevent her friend from leaving even though inwardly she was entreating her to stay. The earl held open the door to allow Maura to leave, and then he stepped inside and closed it behind her before returning his attention to Stacia.

She remembered him as being tall and broad-shouldered. Now he seemed even taller, and his coat fitted perfectly over his well-muscled shoulders. The artifice of padding was not needed to make his coat sit right.

She remained immobile even though she was all too aware of his scrutiny, just as she had been eight years earlier. His gaze had become no less searching. This time it seemed to go right through her shift to the very heart of her, and the strength of her emotions made her oblivious to the immodesty of her situation.

His gaze missed nothing, from the elegant length of her neck, the cleft between her small, high breasts, to her tiny hand-span waist and long, slim legs. When his silent contemplation of her pervaded her feeling of shock, she shivered and something stirred inside her, but whether it was fear or hatred she did not know. It felt like neither, but she shivered all the same, and then she reached out for her shawl and drew it tightly about her.

"My name is Blaise Silverwood," he told her, breaking the silence at last. "I beg your pardon for the intrusion at what is obviously an inconvenient time, but I have wanted to tell you how much I've enjoyed your various performances and had hoped, save for an unfortunate error"—he smiled ironically—"to make your acquaintance before now."

"This is most improper, sir," she said at last, when she was able to tear her gaze away from him.

The smile wavered a little on his lips at so unusual a greeting. This girl displayed none of the simpering and gratitude to which he was accustomed, and he was puzzled.

"I came only to deliver my tribute to your art, ma'am."

"It isn't necessary. We do not act as individuals; we perform as a troupe."

One dark eyebrow rose a little; his lips curved into a faint, ironic smile yet again. Stacia had forgotten the cold. All at once the room felt suffocatingly hot, his closeness oppressing.

"Then my tribute is to the troupe," he responded with a gallantry she hadn't expected, "but I believe you are being unnecessarily modest, Miss Gilbert."

"A condition not often found in actresses."

He ignored her sarcasm to answer gallantly, "It certainly becomes you, ma'am. Regardless of my admiration for your companions, it is you I wish to take to supper."

"I am already engaged."

"On the morrow then."

His presence was threatening to overwhelm her, and she wanted only for him to leave. She had never in her life felt so overcome by emotion in anyone's presence, not even that of Mr. Erasmus Chark, whom she had heartily despised. Not even her dislike of that gentleman caused her brow to perspire, her heart to flutter unevenly in her breast, or her throat to constrict so tightly, she could scarce speak or breathe.

Breathless now, she answered, "I regret it is impossible, sir. You really must leave so I am able to join my companions as we have planned."

His eyes were hooded, masking anything he

might have been feeling at the rebuff as he replied, "The regret is entirely mine, ma'am."

However, Stacia was still able to recognize the puzzlement in his voice, and she understood how he must be feeling. She knew full well he would never have received such a rebuff from a lowly actress before now, moreover one from a troupe of strolling players, most of whom prayed assiduously and often for such a gentleman to come along and perhaps ultimately remove them from a life that was often harsh and degrading and always hard. He wasn't to know that she didn't regard the life as particularly hard. Remaining at Brackentree at her uncle's mercy would have been infinitely worse.

"I'll bid you good night, ma'am," Lord Silverwood was saying, and his manner had become cold, his tone abrupt. "And I wish you good fortune in your endeavors in the future."

Stacia could feel only relief that he was going. In two days' time they would be in Salisbury, and in all likelihood their paths would never cross again. She raised her eyes to look at him directly once again as he moved toward the door, aware that because the amiability in his manner had evaporated, the stiff, formal man before her now was more like the one she recalled so well.

"My lord, you have forgotten your posy. You may take it where it is better appreciated."

He had left it on the dressing table and her words caused him to frown, but he snatched it up as he left the room, and his expression reminded her more of how she remembered him. He'd been angry that day, she now realized. Yes, angry. And yet it was not he who was ruined. She might have told him how, because he had allowed her father to gamble so recklessly and had accepted his vouchers, he had caused her so much grief, but she was sure he did not care enough to feel the slightest regret. Even in his anger at being rebuffed, he had his consolation in Marietta Sanbourne, who would be far more welcoming.

Just as the door closed behind him, Stacia was suddenly galvanized into action, and in her relief she rushed to fully close the door and sank back against it, tears sliding down her cheeks. As the door snapped shut, she heard Mrs. Sanbourne's carrying voice in the corridor.

"Why, Lord Silverwood, what lovely flowers. I'm persuaded you are intent upon spoiling me, so do not seek to deny it. Let us go for supper and allow me to express my gratitude."

Although the earl's voice was deep and melodious, Stacia heard nothing of his reply, and she let out a long breath of blessed relief.

One actress was much like another to the rakes of the beau monde, Stacia told herself, and by the time they reached Salisbury, he would have forgotten all about her. It would take a good deal longer, however, for her to forget about Lord Silverwood.

FOUR

Once again that night Stacia found sleep elusive. For years after she had removed from Dover's End to her uncle's house, the memory of Lord Silverwood's visit had haunted her, although in their severely reduced circumstances her hatred of that young man had been a comfort she' had savored.

Now he had returned, and although he could not possibly know it, the memory of him still came back from time to time to torment her. As she had grown to maturity, so her hatred of him had proportionately increased.

While Maura slept, Stacia found that however hard she tried to blot out her unhappy memories, she could not, and eventually she climbed out of bed, pulled a shawl about her, and crossed the room to peer out of the grimy casement into the street below. Several inebriated gentlemen staggered home while a lightskirt accosted each one with no success. On the hour the watch paused outside to call the time and proclaim all was well.

Since leaving her uncle's house, Stacia had believed all *was* well. She lived in relative poverty, but she was her own woman, and it was a better life than what Uncle Quentin had proposed for her.

As she peered out of the window into a darkness

relieved only by the occasional linkboy and the lamps outside each building, her mind unwillingly returned to that last day she spent at Brackentree, the day of her father's funeral.

Bowed down by her grief, Stacia had found the occasion an almost unbearable ordeal, and as soon as the mourners had left, she slipped away to be alone with her sadness. Outside the immediate family the others who had assembled to pay tribute to Quentin Farramond's scapegrace brother did so only out of respect for her uncle and were mostly strangers who ignored her presence.

Damian had become a man in the years they had lived at Brackentree. The difference in their ages, his frequent absences—first at school and then at Oxford—made it difficult for Stacia to remain close to him, not that they were ever inordinately close. Now with Papa gone she felt she was entirely alone.

The stiff bombazine mourning gown, her first new one since she arrived at Brackentree, felt strange against her skin, but she was comforted in a perverse manner to know that in six months' time her aunt Tess would be obliged to buy her a new mauve one when she went into half-mourning.

It was a great relief when she was at last able to withdraw to her own bedchamber, her refuge on many an occasion since leaving Dover's End. The room was the smallest in the house with the exception of those occupied by the servants, although that did not trouble Stacia in the least. It was still a welcome refuge.

When the family initially went to live at Brackentree, Damian was made somewhat more welcome than Stacia owing to his possessing a substantial allowance from their grandfather's will, something Devin Farramond had been unable to touch, fortunately for her brother.

Because he possessed the Farramond name, an allowance, and dark good looks, he had contrived to marry a local heiress soon after he came down from Oxford. Peggy Asquith was a rather mousy and quiet girl, but Stacia thought she was ideally suited to her brother. When she was first told of their coming nuptials, Stacia started to look forward to the event. Surely after their marriage she would be invited to make her home with Damian and his bride, but no such offer was forthcoming, and from remarks made by the new Mrs. Farramond, Eustacia came to understand she would be welcome to make her home with them only when she was old enough to take charge of the children they hoped to produce. It was a prospect a young lady of Stacia's spirit did not relish, but she supposed it was inevitable. She would, she was bound to acknowledge, exchange being an unpaid servant to her aunt and cousin for a similar position in her brother's household.

So after her father's funeral she felt more desolate than ever. Loose screw and elbow crooker that he had become, he was nevertheless her father, and, in his more sober moments, apt to be affectionate. Now even he was gone, and she allowed the tears of grief to slide down her cheeks, wondering if any happiness would ever be possible for her.

Earlier in the year she had witnessed the marriage of her cousin, Josephine, to a minor member of the aristocracy, a young man who arrived at Brackentree in a yellow-painted curricle that took everyone's eye. Moreover, he was affable and unaffected, treating Stacia in the same cheerful manner as he did everyone else in the household.

On the rare occasions she was allowed to converse with Laurance, Stacia had enjoyed the experience, although she couldn't help feeling a little envious on her cousin's wedding day, wishing wistfully as she sat in the family pew in the local church that one day soon a similar kind of beau would come along and sweep her up, taking her away to their own little house where they could lavish affection upon each other. Sadly she acknowledged that it was all a dream. Without a portion it was unlikely she would be able to make any kind of match.

Up until the day of Josephine's marriage to her beau, Stacia had been carefully discouraged from being in the young man's company, something that had puzzled her a great deal, until she overheard her aunt saying to Uncle Quentin one day, "We must be vigilant with Eustacia, Quentin. That girl is too fetching for her own good."

"She is only a child" was her uncle's disinterested reply, "albeit an expensive one."

"You evidently haven't observed her of late. She is all but a woman."

"That is no reason to be blue-deviled, my dear." Stacia knew she should not be eavesdropping on the conversation but mitigated her action by the very fact they were talking about her. "A fair countenance might enable us to find her a good match. It would discharge our responsibility for the chit."

"With no portion and an independent mind, I fear you are casting stones against the wind, Quentin. Gentlemen do not like intemperate females, and

36

Eustacia can be a hornet when the mood is upon her."

"Oh, I don't know. . . ."

"In any event consider the expense."

"Perhaps one of our tenant farmers," Mr. Farramond mused. "Trewindle was widowed last year and has a brood of tiny children to care for. I know he would welcome a wife, even one who occasionally flies up into the boughs."

"That is as may be. Just for now we must keep her away from Laurance when he calls. He remarked to Josephine only the other day that her cousin was ravishingly beautiful. Your daughter, poor child, was most put-out."

Stacia had been outraged at the tone of the conversation, for however much she liked Laurance and envied Josephine her coming nuptials, she had never looked upon the young man as anything other than a friendly face.

That evening when she was about to retire to bed, she took the opportunity of examining herself carefully in the pier glass. Stacia was persuaded Laurance meant only to curry favor with Josephine when he described her cousin as ravishingly beautiful, and she really wondered what it was to be fetching, but she realized as she gazed at her reflection in the glass that her figure was now as fine as any other young lady's of her acquaintance, her skin flawlessly pale, her hair a deep, burnished brown, and her eyes wide and dark, luminous in the flickering candlelight. Much good it would do her, she thought when she turned away and began to prepare for bed.

Stacia had been in her room for only a short

time, indulging in her grief privately, when her aunt came to find her.

"So here you are," she said, her face set into a disapproving expression. "Why are you lurking in your room?"

"I waited until all the visitors had left."

As Stacia hastily wiped away her tears, her aunt scolded, "Just look at you, child. Your eyes are red and puffy. You'll be obliged to ask Cook for some cucumber, but later. Your uncle wishes to speak with you in the library. Immediately."

Stacia looked up sharply. It could not be about her father's will; Devin Farramond had left nothing. Ever since losing to Lord Silverwood, Devin Farramond had been without a rag, reliant upon the grudging charity of his brother.

"What is it about, Aunt?"

Mrs. Farramond clucked her tongue. "Now, now, Eustacia. It is not for you to ask, child. Just go and obey unquestioningly for once, if you please, but first wash your face. We don't want . . ."

She bit her lip and Stacia looked at her curiously. "Yes, Aunt?"

Mrs. Farramond hurried toward the door. "Just do as you are bid—in a brace of snaps!"

A few minutes later Stacia entered the library, where a welcoming fire was lit in the hearth. That in itself was surprising, for it was March, and although a chill wind still blew, Uncle Quentin regarded the winter as over and ordered fires only in the drawing room after dinner and in the kitchen for cooking. Stacia often found her way to the kitchen to enjoy the warmth of it as well as the companionship of the servants.

"Ah, there you are, Eustacia!" Quentin Farramond greeted her in a hearty manner his niece found puzzling.

"Uncle Quentin, I am told you wish to see me."

As she approached, she became aware that he was not alone: a pair of stockinged legs were thrust toward the fire.

"Sad day, m'dear," murmured Mr. Erasmus Chark as he sipped at a glass of madeira. "Sad day. We all feel for your loss."

Erasmus Chark was a familiar figure in the Farramond household, a crony of her uncle, local magistrate, master of hounds and occupant of the Manor, a few miles from Brackentree. Whenever Stacia found herself in his company, she was invariably polite, but she could not like him, nor his unkempt and grubby appearance, nor did she enjoy the way he always found his way to her side, or his habit of touching her arm and cheek in what she considered an overfamiliar manner.

"Eustacia, my dear," her uncle began, and his unease transmitted itself to her. "I know your grief is deep and, therefore, I believe it the correct time to make a move that is bound to bring you a measure of happiness." She kept on looking at him with the direct gaze her aunt often called insolent, but Mr. Farramond was forced to avert his eyes from hers, looking toward the fire as he went on, "Last year Damian tied the knot with dear Peggy, and Josephine is enjoying nuptial bliss with Laurance. . . ."

All at once Stacia had visions of Wilf Trewindle, the coarse farmer, with his brood of children. It was generally held in the community that he had outworn his wife and she had welcomed her untimely demise as a blessed relief from her earthly bur-

39

dens. Stacia's resolve hardened. She would have none of it, however persuasive Uncle Quentin tried to be.

Mr. Chark peered into his glass. His nose and cheeks were ruddy, and Stacia didn't doubt he had already consumed a great deal of madeira, using her father's funeral as justification, as if he needed one in order to imbibe. Gentlemen, with their all-consuming passion for drink and gaming, she thought contemptuously.

Mr. Farramond cleared his throat. "I'll not mince words with you, Eustacia. Mr. Chark has kindly offered for you, my dear."

Stacia stared at her uncle in blank disbelief. "Mr. Chark."

The announcement shocked her to the core, for she had not envisaged such a thing. Erasmus Chark was as old as her father, perhaps older.

"He is willing to take you as his wife without a portion, which is handsome of him. Eustacia, I do trust you are sensible of the honor Mr. Chark is bestowing upon you."

"Mr. Chark," she repeated, still disbelieving.

Like most young ladies, Stacia had an image of the man she would one day marry. Long ago she had decided he would be nothing like the gentlemen with whom she was already acquainted. He would be fair of face, with blue eyes that were always laughing, and although he must possess an authoritative manner, he would also be indulgent of her. Where she might encounter such a gentleman, especially with her lack of means, Stacia had no notion, but it was her dream.

"We'll have a merry old time," Mr. Chark told her, and he chuckled heartily at the prospect. "I have it in mind you and I will deal very well together, my dear."

"No, we will not," she retorted, finding her voice at last.

A good deal of her uncle's bonhomie faded at this point. "Eustacia, must I remind you to mind your manners?"

Mr. Chark chuckled again, and as he did so, some of the madeira spilled down the front of his shirt and his old-fashioned brocade waistcoat. "I like a spirited filly, Farramond. Didn't I tell you so? They break down to the most placid of mounts, don't you know!"

Stacia cast him a disgusted look and then transferred her attention to her uncle once again. "I'm sorry, Uncle, but marriage to Mr. Chark is entirely out of the question."

"Let me remind you, girl, I am your legal guardian. It is I who decides what is best for you."

"If that is so, I must respectfully point out your judgment is totally wanting."

"Flesh and fire!" Mr. Chark retorted, slapping his knee with his free hand. "We *will* have a merry old time of it."

"How dare a mere snip of a girl cast doubt on my judgment!" Mr. Farramond roared, and then, casting an uneasy glance at his friend, tempered his manner. "My dear, the past few days have been trying upon all of us, so I will overlook what can only be your blue devils. Mr. Chark also understands your feelings at this time. . . ."

Stacia drew herself up to her full height, although she still presented a diminutive figure. She wished at that moment that she could appear more imposing. "If only he did," she responded, "for if it

41

were so, he would be fully aware I have no intention of marrying him or anyone of your choosing, sir. Moreover, I believe it's true to say you wouldn't dare to treat me in this utterly odious manner if Papa were still alive."

Mr. Farramond's face grew purple with rage. "I won't tolerate this disobedience. Let there be no more discussion on the matter, which is already settled."

"You can't—" she began to protest, but her uncle went on regardless, "Your wedding is arranged for Friday week."

"This is a trick and a half!" Stacia protested, and then, turning to the would-be bridegroom, "Mr. Chark, I implore you, inform my uncle you have no wish for an unwilling bride."

" 'Tis only your modesty, my dear, that prompts this outburst, nothing more," the old man replied. "You will come about. Just you see if you don't."

"This is outside of enough!" she cried, and then her uncle informed her, "The wedding will be a quiet affair due to the current circumstances. . . ."

"And the bride wore black!" she cried, turning on her heel and rushing out of the room, only to have her arm caught by her aunt, who had been listening at the door.

"Ingrate!" she accused. "You are in no position to turn down a respectable offer."

"There is no reasoning with any of you," Stacia said in desperation before tearing herself away from Mrs. Farramond's grip.

She rushed up the stairs, almost stumbling several times before she reached her own room, and after she had slammed the door shut, she threw herself headlong across the bed with sobs racking her body.

The matter of her prospective marriage would not go away—Stacia knew that all too well. Uncle Quentin was accustomed to being obeyed in all things, and she needed no telling that he was anxious to be rid of his responsibility for her. However, she was not prepared for the effect her stand would have. The next few days were a nightmare, for all members of the household were instructed not to speak to her, nor was she to be welcomed to the table, and only bread and water were to be served to her.

Stacia scarcely missed conversing with her aunt and uncle, and her appetite was such that bread and water were more than sufficient to sustain her. After three days, during which she refused to be cowed into submission, Damian arrived at Brackentree and she welcomed him effusively, seeing in him a potential savior of the situation.

"Oh, Damian, my dear, I am so glad to see you! I have been obliged to endure the most disagreeable time."

"What is this Uncle Quentin tells me of your obstinacy?" was her brother's unsympathetic response to her problem.

"Obstinacy!" she echoed. "Damian, Uncle Quentin wishes me to marry Erasmus Chark! The wedding is planned for next week. Do you truly expect me to be in high snuff at the prospect?"

His gaze slid away from her. "You could do worse, Eustacia. Old Chark is as rich as Golden Ball."

She turned away from him and covered her face with her hands. "Not you, too, Damian. I looked to you for support. I thought you might help me."

"I am not your guardian. Uncle Quentin is. There is little I can do."

"You can't possibly agree with him."

"Not precisely, but you've got to be a realist. You don't have many options available to you."

Stacia allowed her hands to drop and she straightened up, gazing out of the window without seeing anything but the blackness of her own future. "No, I don't suppose I do," she acknowledged at last.

His relief was almost palpable, and encouraged by what he saw as her compliance, he came up to her and put his hands on her arms. "It might not be the case of pickles you envisage. Old Chark is full of juice, you know, and with a bit of good fortune you might find yourself a wealthy widow before long."

His words, meant to comfort her, served only to make her laugh harshly, and when he left Brackentree a little while later, he was confident he had instilled some sense into his sister's mind.

After his departure Stacia spent most of her time pacing her room or walking in the garden in an effort to find some resolution to her problem. However much her family conspired against her, she was determined not to be swayed, but she was no longer so certain she could remain unyielding.

A few days after Damian's visit she watched the Farramond carriage depart for dinner at her brother's house. She had not been asked to join them— not that she had wanted to. The atmosphere would be too strained and her sister-in-law unlikely to be any more sympathetic than all the other members of the family.

In the past Stacia had tolerated Erasmus Chark as a friend of her uncle's with no liking but with a certain amount of amusement. Since his offer of marriage she knew that even being in the same room with him would make her feel ill.

As soon as she lost sight of her uncle's carriage, she slipped downstairs to the kitchen. Cook was baking bread for the weekend, and as soon as she saw Stacia, she broke off, cut a large chunk of the freshly baked bread, spread it thickly with butter, and brought some cheese out of the cold room.

"I'm not supposed to do this," she said as Stacia sat down at the table.

"Then you should not, Mrs. Stubbings. I don't want you to get into any trouble on my behalf."

"Eat it and welcome. You look as if you need the sustenance. You've not an ounce of flesh on your bones."

She poured out a glass of lemonade as Stacia laughed hollowly. "I shall need more than this to sustain me if I'm to marry Mr. Chark."

"Disgustin', that's what we call it. Such an old gentleman and so uncouth, and you barely sixteen. It's not right. All of us belowstairs think so."

"My uncle doesn't share our opinion of Mr. Chark, and I fear it is his view that matters."

All at once Stacia found herself hungry, and she began to devour the food Cook had put before her. When she had finished, a large portion of apple pie appeared and she ate that, too, piled high with clotted cream.

"What's goin' to 'appen, Miss Eustacia?" Cook asked. "We're all that worried about you."

Stacia sat back in the chair and drew a profound sigh. "I can think of no good solution to the problem, however much I rack my brains. If I could find some means to run away, I would," she added, "but I haven't ninepence to bless myself with, so I cannot realistically entertain that consideration. I know if I had sufficient funds to get to London, I'd be able to find a position as a governess or companion. I know I would."

"London's the devil's own place," Cook told her. "Sinful goin's-on, I'm told."

Stacia was forced to laugh. "I daresay."

She thought of Lord Silverwood for the first time in years. If London was the devil's own place, then he would be perfectly at home there.

"I'd liefer make a pact with the devil than marry Erasmus Chark," she retorted as she accepted another piece of the pie.

"That's sinful talk, that is," Cook scolded, "but you're beyond reason, there's no doubtin', and who can blame you, in all conscience?"

The butler had come into the kitchen, and he and Cook exchanged meaningful glances. A moment later Cook took a few coins out of her apron pocket and laid them on the table.

Stacia looked up at her questioningly, and the woman explained, "Just some pin money, Miss Eustacia. Take it if it helps and welcome."

Stacia got to her feet. "I cannot take your money, Mrs. Stubbings. You have little enough without giving it to me."

"Don't trouble your head on our behalf, ma'am. It's little enough in truth. I only wish there was more. There'll just be a little less in the vicar's plate on Sunday."

Stacia grinned. "*Now* who is being sinful?"

Cook looked bashful, and then Mr. Grindle, the butler, added to the coins with some of his own. "It might just get you to where you want to be, somewhere a mite more hospitable than this."

"I really don't know what to say. This might just save my life."

"You can always repay us when you're up in the stirrups."

"You may be sure I will repay it with interest!" Stacia vowed. "God bless the both of you."

"We'll miss you," Cook told her. "There's never been anything stiff-rumped about you." Then, after hesitating for a moment, she asked, "Do you really intend to go?"

Stacia considered for a moment or two before she sighed and said, "Yes, I must, now that you have made it possible. It would be folly to remain and endure more Turkish treatment."

"When?" asked Mr. Grindle. "When do you intend to go?"

Stacia turned to look at him. "Now. I believe I shall go now."

"But it's coming onto evening, Miss Eustacia," Mr. Grindle pointed out, looking shocked.

"I don't relish going out into the unknown, but I must go now or lose my confidence."

"I'll pack up some cheese and oatcakes," Cook told her, but Stacia was already out of the kitchen and on her way to pack a few necessary belongings in a cloak bag.

The prospect of going unprotected into the

harsh world beyond the gates of Brackentree was a frightening one, but it was, she knew without a doubt, preferable to marriage to Erasmus Chark.

FIVE

The shabby carriage swayed and creaked as it made its plodding way from Dorrington toward Salisbury. Stacia couldn't help but feel relieved Dorrington was behind her. She would remember her engagement there, and not because it was the place she had enjoyed her first professional acclaim.

"I am delighted to inform you, my dears," Ormerod Greaves declared, "we have just enjoyed our best-ever week for as long as I am able to recall, and we are engaged to appear in Dorrington again in September. Good news indeed!"

He beamed at each occupant in turn, expecting them to mirror his pleasure. Stacia did force herself to return his smile, comforted in some small measure by the knowledge that Dorrington had been, that week, the venue of a fight between two pugilists of renown. It was, no doubt, what had brought Lord Silverwood and his cronies to so rustic a spot. It was just an unfortunate coincidence she happened to be appearing there and one that was hardly likely to occur again.

"I have it in mind *Othello* will be well received in Salisbury," Marietta Sanbourne murmured.

"Yes, indeed, my dear. I'm persuaded my performance of the Moor will be the best ever."

"Do you recall, Ormerod, how well we were received when last we played in Salisbury?" Mrs. Sanbourne asked, her demeanor becoming more animated.

"It was your portrayal of Desdemona that caused the ruction."

"A lady swooned in the gallery, and a young buck proposed marriage."

Marietta Sanbourne continued to smile at the memory, and Maura looked meaningfully across the carriage to Stacia, who sank back against the squabs, lost in her own thoughts. She was beginning to take a more reasonable attitude to her encounter with the earl. Distressing as it was, she understood at last she had no reason to fear him. There was nothing more he could do to add to her stock of misery, but she did fear discovery. Beyond the first heady aftermath of her triumph, she acknowledged she could not afford to become renowned as an actress. That would invite too much scrutiny, and as her uncle was still her legal guardian and would remain so until she came of age in two years' time, it would be better if she stayed unknown. Until that day it was still possible for Uncle Quentin to find her, return her to Brackentree, and force her to marry Erasmus Chark.

"We must propose a vote of thanks to Stacia for our excellent reception in Dorrington," Maura sought to remind them.

Stacia smiled shyly as Mr. Greaves declared, "No one would seek to deny Miss Gilbert her rightful dues, Mrs. Copeland."

"My dear Miss Gilbert, you are yet a beginner in the thespian arts," Mrs. Sanbourne told her. "You mustn't allow a little applause to make you strut like a crow in a gutter."

Stacia snapped out of her reminiscences, but before she could think of a suitably stinging reply, Maura retorted, "Stacia would never do that, ma'am. Her head is not so easily turned, unlike others who are less worthy of the acclaim they receive."

Marietta Sanbourne drew in a sharp breath, and Mr. Greaves cut in before a full-scale argument could ensue. "Ladies, let us have no brangling, if you please. It is most unseemly, and as we have a long journey ahead of us, we should at least attempt to complete it as amicably as possible. We all play our parts as equal members of this company. None has precedence over the other."

Stacia cast him a grateful smile. She was fond of Ormerod Greaves, who had somehow never fulfilled his potential as an actor, unlike Mr. Kean or Mr. Kemble, but he was good at heart and insisted upon sharing equally their sometimes meager rewards. Stacia regarded him as her savior. If it hadn't been for Ormerod Greaves, she didn't know what might have become of her after she left Brackentree. . . .

It had taken her little time to pack a few essentials in a cloak bag on that fateful evening. Her uncle and aunt were not free with their money, grudging what had to be spent on necessities, and Damian had developed into a clutchfist, too. She supposed it was better than her father's inability to hold on to his money or his property, but she felt there must be some middle ground.

Before leaving, she decided to change out of her severe black gown. A young lady dressed in deepest

51

mourning would attract too much attention. Although she did experience a little pang of conscience for betraying her father's memory so soon after his demise, she felt sure he would have understood. Those last few years, when he was subjected to Uncle Quentin's disapproving charity, had been difficult for him, too, and so his drinking increased, hastening his demise.

When she had finished putting together her few belongings, the servants watched, grim-faced, as she left, and she was aware she could rely upon their discretion when her disappearance was discovered. As she trudged toward the main road, she hoped her aunt and uncle wouldn't discover her missing until the morrow. Not being welcome at their table for meals now proved an advantage to her.

After a while she lost track of how long she had walked—suffice it to say her feet began to feel considerably sore—but now that she had made the decision to leave Brackentree, there was no going back. No future perils could be worse than marriage to Erasmus Chark.

Just when she thought she could walk no further, a farm wagon came into sight, and she clambered aboard the turnips with no thought for the indignity of her position. The farmer was bound for market with his produce. A ride to the next market town was exactly what she had hoped for when she set out. It would enable her to catch the first stage that came to the posting inn. Considering a possible pursuit, she reckoned that Uncle Quentin would never be able to find her now. With that particular anxiety lifted from her mind, she sank back into the sacks of turnips and carrots and fell fast asleep.

When she awoke, it was with a start because of the jolting of the cart as it came to a standstill. For a brief moment or two Stacia wondered where she could be, but then she opened her eyes fully to discover they had stopped in a bustling market square. It was still very early in the morning, much earlier than gentlefolk normally ventured out, but the farmers were already doing brisk business.

Still rather sleepy, Stacia climbed down, and when she tipped the farmer a vail of a precious sixpence out of her meager funds, he directed her to the posting inn across the market square. The Swan and Talbot she saw was but a few yards from where they had stopped, and waving airily to her Good Samaritan, she went to inquire of the landlord about the arrival of the next stagecoach.

To her surprise the public rooms of the inn were as busy as the marketplace itself. Would-be travelers were eating, drinking, and talking all at once. Children mewled on their mothers' knees. The noise was so tremendous, Stacia could only stand and marvel. When some of the gentlemen began to take an interest in her, she quickly went to find the innkeeper. To her utter dismay he shook his head as he perused the waybill.

"Sorry, miss, there's not a place to be had on any of the mornin' stages. Everyone wants to travel today. Never seen the like, I confess to you."

"I don't mind riding outside, or in the basket, or even what destination, but I must leave Kidlington today."

He subjected her to such a curious look, Stacia was sorry to have sounded so desperate. She real-

53

ized she had made it obvious she was a runaway. It was a great mistake, but she could do nothing to put matters to rights now.

All she did was bite her lip as he answered unsympathetically, "Don't see 'ow it's possible, miss." His eyes narrowed, suddenly shifty. " 'Less you wants to hire a post chaise. I've got one available at a price."

"I don't have the means," she answered truthfully.

"I've nothin' afore tomorrow mornin', then."

Stacia was just about to protest that it was too late when she stilled her tongue. By tomorrow morning Uncle Quentin could have visited every posting inn in the county. She had to be on the morning stage if she was to stand any chance of retaining her freedom, and she had a strange feeling the innkeeper was well aware of her dilemma.

However, before she could voice a protest, the fellow was called away, and she sank back against the wall and closed her eyes, giving in at last to her despair. Surely life wasn't always going to be this cruel to her. Dame Fortune had to smile upon her one day. Today would be as good a time as any, she thought.

When she opened her eyes again, a movement outside caught her attention. Through the window Stacia saw Damian climbing down from the natty little curricle his wife had bought for him on the occasion of their marriage. With it went a team of the finest—and fastest—matched chestnuts.

"No!" she breathed, her eyes wide with alarm.

Even aware of the possibility of pursuit, she had not expected it so soon. Despite the imminence of being apprehended like a common felon, she was

54

determined not to be returned to Brackentree in disgrace and treated like an inanimate object with no feelings or considerations, to be disposed of as Uncle Quentin wished.

Apart from the door through which Damian would come at any moment, there was only one other avenue of escape, and without a moment's thought Stacia pushed it open and rushed into a room, where she found several pairs of eyes turned upon her in surprise. Her flight came to an immediate halt just inside the doorway, where she stood immobile and wide-eyed with fear.

It was immediately apparent she had burst in on a private parlor and a group of people having breakfast. One of the group, a gentleman, got to his feet as she entered the room. He was a large man, built like a bear, and when he spoke, his voice boomed out, startling her even further.

"Madam, to what do we owe the undoubted pleasure of your company?"

"I . . ." she began, her mind feverishly seeking a convincing explanation for her presence.

Beyond the door, in the corridor outside, she heard the innkeeper say, "Thank you kindly, sir. I am most obliged to you," and Stacia groaned inwardly, imagining Damian tipping him a vail. "The young lady was certainly 'ere a few moments ago. She cannot have gone far. I 'ad her tagged as a runaway the moment I clapped eyes on 'er."

Even as he spoke, the parlor door began to open. As it did so, Stacia instinctively slipped behind it, aware that only a few inches away her brother was scouring the room in search of her. She even held her breath so that he could not hear her labored breathing.

"Sir, what is the meaning of this intrusion?" the man Stacia soon came to know as Ormerod Greaves demanded, drawing himself up to his full, not inconsiderable, height.

Again she held her breath, fearful that she would be betrayed by these people, who knew nothing of her situation.

"Landlord!" Mr. Greaves boomed before Damian could reply. "Is this a private parlor or is it not?"

"My hearty apologies, sir," she heard Damian say, and as the door closed behind him, Stacia let out a sigh of relief the others were bound to notice.

"Thank you, sir," she told him. "A few moments more of your indulgence and I shall disturb you no longer."

"My name is Greaves," he told her. "Ormerod Greaves, and this is Mrs. Sanbourne, Mrs. Copeland, and young Master Dalton. You might find it more pleasant to remain in here with us for now. Come and take a little breakfast with us, child," he invited.

"Thank you, no, sir. . . ."

"She's a runaway, Ormerod," Mrs. Sanbourne warned him. "Why did you not tell that nice young man she was here?"

"We are all running away, Marietta," he responded, "and in any event he did not ask. Come, ma'am, and sit by the fire. I shall pour you a cup of coffee, and you must help yourself to some food. There is more than enough, as you can see. The landlord for all his failings has been most hospitable to a troupe of strolling players."

That certainly explained his expansive voice and extravagant gestures, which made Stacia smile faintly. She nodded in acknowledgment as he went

56

on to introduce the other people present, but she did not supply her own name in return.

When Mr. Greaves gesticulated toward the half-empty plates and dishes, Stacia continued to hesitate but then decided she was in no position to refuse the offer of a meal. She had no notion when the next one might be available, or how much transport was likely to cost her.

As she turned toward the table bearing the food, the gentleman who had so far been doing all the talking explained, "Our company is called the Gala Troupe. You may have heard of us."

"I regret, sir, my acquaintance with the theater is not great. My uncle, with whom I have lived for several years, did not approve of such visits."

"In that case I do not in the least blame you for leaving."

"I'll wager that is not her reason for leaving, Ormerod," the woman told him, and Stacia decided she did not in the least like Mrs. Sanbourne's jaundiced attitude.

"Why *did* you leave?" the cheeky young lad asked.

"Billy, that is none of your business," Mr. Greaves responded.

Stacia shot him a grateful smile, and when she had filled a plate with a selection from the cold collation, Maura Copeland moved along the bench to make room for her.

"This is most kind of you," Stacia told them, averting her eyes from all the curious ones watching her. "I really am grateful to you all."

"We've just had an excellent week. Mrs. Sanbourne has been received very well with audiences with her portrayal of Lady Macbeth."

"I have read the play," Stacia confessed, "and I imagine it is a difficult part."

"Not for me, dear," Mrs. Sanbourne told her. "It is a great pity you have not been privileged to see me in the part. It would have been a revelation to you."

"Oh, indeed," Stacia agreed as she consumed the food with great relish.

"When she played Juliet, there wasn't a dry eye in the house," another member of the company informed her.

Stacia glanced at the actress then and acknowledged whereas she must once have been a beauty, her looks were a little faded now. The thought that this big bear of a man was her likely Romeo almost made Stacia laugh out loud, but then she felt guilty because of his kindness to her.

"Where are you bound?" Maura Copeland asked when Stacia had finished the welcome repast.

"I had been hoping to catch the morning stage to London, but the innkeeper tells me it is full and there is no further transportation until the morrow."

"That is indeed a pity," Mr. Greaves replied.

"I'll wager it is more than a pity," Mrs. Sanbourne scoffed.

"You speak well for yourself," Mr. Greaves observed. "Have you ever acted?"

Stacia stared at him in amazement before she replied, "Only when very young—with my brother."

"There is a family resemblance," Marietta Sanbourne said, not troubling to hide the malice in her tone.

"I don't suppose you would regard it as acting," Stacia explained. "More like children's games to amuse their elders."

58

"Do you sing perchance a little?" Mr. Greaves persisted.

"Yes, certainly, a little to my own accompaniment, naturally. I have learned to play the pianoforte."

"Heaven preserve us from bread-and-butter misses," Mrs. Sanbourne whispered loud enough for Stacia to hear.

Ormerod Greaves turned to look at his colleague. "This young lady could be an asset to us, Marietta."

The actress sat up straight, crying, "Oh, really! What humbug you speak, Ormerod!"

"Why don't you join our troupe?" he asked Stacia then, ignoring entirely his colleague's disdain.

Stacia looked bewildered. "Are you asking me to join a company of traveling actors, sir?"

"It's beneath your dignity, I suppose," Mrs. Sanbourne sniffed.

"No, no," Stacia hastened to assure her. "It's merely that I have no experience or aptitude."

"That is of no account," Mrs. Copeland told her. "Experience is gained as we go. I was a seamstress till my Albert was killed at Salamanca, so now I make costumes and play minor roles. This way I don't starve. Well, not often anyway."

"You're behaving like a clunch, Ormerod," Marietta Sanbourne continued to scoff. "To this young lady being an actress is akin to becoming a Paphian."

"That is the opinion of many gentlefolk," Maura Copeland told her, "even though they are the ones who enjoy theater the most."

"Oh, no," Stacia hastened to assure them. "I don't share that opinion in the least."

59

In truth she had never given the matter a moment's thought.

"One of our most promising protégées," Ormerod Greaves explained as Marietta Sanbourne continued to look disapproving, "left us to become leg-shackled to an ostler we met on the road."

"Promising!" Mrs. Sanbourne scoffed. "Quite the amateur, I say."

The big man ignored her and continued to address Stacia. "What do you say, Miss . . . ?"

"Stacia," she supplied quickly, and then added her mother's maiden name. "My name is Stacia Gilbert."

"Miss Gilbert, I can offer you a small share of our earnings, whatever it happens to be. It will not, in any event, be a princely sum, I am bound to confess to you, and although it's a hard life at times, your duties won't be too onerous. A little sewing, prompting, and the like. Mayhap the small role now and again if we feel you are capable." While she hesitated to reply, he added, "You don't have to stay with us if you don't like the life. We're on our way to Exeter for a week's engagement. You can always reconsider your position after that."

Exeter, Stacia thought. She wasn't exactly sure where it was, but she fancied it was a long way from Brackentree.

"Ormerod, the chit's not out of the schoolroom," Mrs. Sanbourne pointed out. "We could be charged with kidnapping and thrown into the bridewell. Why *did* you run away?"

"To escape an arranged marriage," Stacia countered angrily. "I had no taste for the man chosen for me."

"La!" Mrs. Sanbourne scoffed. "You may come to

regret your impetuosity, my girl. It's a cruel world without the protection of a husband."

"That is a gamble I am willing to take, ma'am."

"This is just wasting time," Ormerod Greaves broke in irritably. "We need another to join us if we are to function efficiently. Miss Gilbert speaks well, and I like her enunciation."

"I believe you have taken leave of your senses, Ormerod. The chit mutters," the actress complained. "I do hope she is not a felon to boot."

"I am not!" Stacia protested, losing some of her fearfulness at last and growing weary of the woman's constant carping.

"It would not be like playing charades in some country house, madam," she persisted.

"No doubt it is more enjoyable."

"It's a hard grind sometimes," Maura Copeland told her soberly. "Not at all the life for cosset lambs."

Stacia felt this woman, who bore none of Marietta Sanbourne's haughtiness or false sense of worth, was evidently trying to be kind.

She thought fleetingly of her years of fetching and carrying for an ungrateful aunt and an often spiteful cousin and replied at last, "As you've observed, I have lived in a comfortable manner all my life, but I am also accustomed to hard work. If I do it among felicitous company, ma'am, I shall not mind it in the least."

When she had finished speaking, Stacia thought she detected a spark of sympathy in Maura Copeland's eyes and warmed to her. As for Marietta Sanbourne, Stacia felt that there was no real malice behind her blustering, and common sense told her that if she traveled to Exeter with these people,

Damian or Uncle Quentin would never be able to find her.

"I accept your offer, sir," she answered at last. "If I do not suit after an initial period, we can part with no regrets on either side."

"It's a bargain!" Ormerod Greaves cried, and then, turning to the others, he declared, "Come along, my dears. We have delayed long enough. We must be on our way if we're to reach Exeter by nightfall. We cannot afford the expense of hiring a linkboy to accompany us."

Marietta Sanbourne rose to her feet with a gentle majesty and began to button up her shabby pelisse. Fixing Stacia with a meaningful glare, she swept out of the room, saying, "I do hope you will not live to regret this, Ormerod."

Many performances later, graduating from maid-of-all work to nonspeaking roles, to minor ones and then to the major parts Marietta Sanbourne was unable to tackle—those of young girls—Stacia eyed the older woman curiously, wondering if her own recent successes had made her regret the engagement of an ingenue even more. She suspected that Mrs. Sanbourne would not give up her position as principal in the troupe easily, nor did Stacia wish her to do so. She had little ambition, despite the way she had taken to the life with such ease. All she had wanted was a roof over her head at night and sufficient food to sustain her, at least until she came of age, when she would truly be her own woman. Those wishes had not changed in the meantime.

"You must regret leaving Dorrington, Mrs. Sanbourne," Maura ventured.

"I don't see why you would think so," the woman

replied. "Dorrington is a rustic place, and the audience is quite unable to discern what is good and bad in theater." This last comment was directed at Stacia, who chose to ignore it.

Maura affected an innocent air. "I was not thinking of our performances in the theater, ma'am, merely of your new relationship with Lord Silverwood."

The mere mention of that gentleman's name was sufficient to make Stacia stiffen. If Marietta Sanbourne knew of his villainy, would she care? she asked herself. No doubt she would not. Lord Silverwood was wealthy—as rich as Croesus, so they said. An aging actress would only hope for such a man to come along and install her in a life of luxury and ease. Stacia could not blame her for that wish. There were times when she, too, desired fresh, clean linen on which to rest her head at night, scented bathwater on demand, and an army of servants to bring her whatever her heart desired. It had once been so, but no more, and she didn't waste her time on useless dreams.

Maura's words, however, had a startling effect upon Marietta Sanbourne, who began to smile foolishly. The other members of the company often voiced their curiosity about the long-gone Mr. Sanbourne. It was rumored that Billy, the callboy, was her son, but as the actress herself never commented on the matter, no one else dared to broach the subject.

"Lord Silverwood belongs in Dorrington no more than I, Maura," the actress answered smugly. "I have no doubt he will seek me out wherever I may be. He is the kind of man who would travel the length and breadth of the earth to win the heart of his chosen one."

She sighed in such a profound manner that Stacia was obliged to look away.

"Do tell us, ma'am," Maura persisted, and Stacia noted the mischievous gleam in her eye, "all about his lordship. How did he divert you?"

"We enjoyed a most superb supper, consisting of the finest foodstuffs and sweetmeats money can buy."

"And afterward, ma'am?" Maura persisted.

"This is an impudence, Mrs. Copeland," Mr. Greaves told her, and his face became dark. "You mustn't press Mrs. Sanbourne on the details of her private life."

"Oh, I do beg pardon for being so curious," Maura responded, looking not in the least regretful, "but supper with a member of the haut ton is something of a mystery to the likes of us, sir, and will probably always remain one."

"Quite so," Marietta agreed, looking pleased again. "It is a great pity you two ladies were not privileged to become acquainted with him, although it is not like he would have noticed you. Only leading ladies are like to catch his eye. He has his own box at both Drury Lane and Covent Garden, you know. Such a gentleman is unlike to come your way, and in all humility, I pity you for it."

Stacia felt Maura shake against her. She began to cough, and Stacia was only too well aware she was hiding her laughter. If only they were discussing any other gentleman, Stacia knew she would be equally amused by this woman's pretensions.

"Such a gentleman." Mrs. Sanbourne sighed yet

again. "He was all condescension and consideration to me."

Ormerod Greaves began to shuffle some papers noisily. "I think we should while away our time perfecting our roles until we stop for dinner. None of us can afford to lessen our efforts if we are to enjoy supper without the aid of an aristocratic gentleman."

Stacia smiled at last, for she had come to suspect during her association with the company that Mr. Greaves harbored a fancy for his leading lady. However, she realized Marietta Sanbourne would never succumb to Ormerod Greaves while she still dreamed of a season at Drury Lane and gentlemen like the Earl of Silverwood dancing attendance on her.

Ormerod Greaves handed out their lines, and when Stacia glanced at the title of their main offering for Exeter, she was forced to smile yet again. *The Devilish Earl.* What irony. It was so apt. The play couldn't be a better one. As the object of the evil nobleman's desire, Stacia felt she would give the performance of a lifetime.

SIX

The applause was still ringing in her ears when
Stacia went to her dressing room to change. It had
been a triumphant week at the Theatre Royal,
Manchester, and she glowed from the pleasure of
knowing she was a positive asset to the company. It
was worth tolerating a little envious carping from
some of the other females in the troupe, for her success, as they all appreciated, was for the benefit of
them all. In any event apart from Ormerod, Marietta, Maura, Billy, and herself, other members of
the troupe came and went with monotonous regu-
larity.

Recently she had become accustomed to returning to her dressing room to find several gifts of
sweetmeats and flowers from admirers. It was no
longer a novelty for her to receive admiration. She
read all the cards that accompanied the gifts. Many
of them begged a meeting and offered to take her to
supper. She always ignored such requests. Any
gifts of value, such as jewelry, were returned with
a polite note, to the disgust of Marietta Sanbourne,
who began to call her, not unkindly, "the Nun."

"Your attic's to let if you refuse all offers," the
older actress had told her recently.

"Yes, I daresay" was Stacia's good-humored reply,
"but my acquaintanceship can only be fleeting, for

we move on at the end of the week. It happened between you and Lord Silverwood, I recall."

Marietta Sanbourne was unperturbed by the mention of his name. "It is still possible for a meeting to lead to a wonderful life."

"It is not what I want, Mrs. Sanbourne. I don't wish to be at the mercy of a man's generosity and whims."

"Tush! Such modern thinking is beyond my comprehension! Do you wish to remain a traveling actor for the rest of your life?"

Stacia didn't answer, for in truth she did not know. Fortunately Ormerod usually scolded Marietta, saying, "You chucklehead! Hold your tongue. Stacia is our greatest asset. Do you want to lose her?"

At this point Stacia always assured him of her wish to stay with the Gala Troupe, whatever temptations came her way.

Before Maura could start to unfasten Stacia's gown, the door opened and Ormerod Greaves stood in the aperture.

"My dear, you were divine! Simply divine! You have made the role of Dorabella your own, you know. *The Devilish Earl* would not work with another in the leading role."

"Thank you, sir," Stacia replied shyly.

In the two years that had passed since her encounter with Lord Silverwood in Dorrington, the fortunes of the Gala Troupe had improved immeasurably. They now played at major provincial theaters and were able to lodge in decent houses, eating well at every meal. Stacia tried not to allow the knowledge that she was in good measure responsible for their recent successes to turn her head.

Marietta Sanbourne still played weightier roles, but she and Ormerod bowed to the inevitability that it was Stacia who brought in the crowds and that her success in doing so was for the benefit of them all.

It was a heady feeling for Stacia to know she could reduce a grown man to tears with the pathos of her role and make him roar with laughter a short time later. The fact that she had now come of age was a bonus, for if her fame was to spread and Uncle Quentin came to know of the life she was leading, it wouldn't matter a jot. To her great relief his hold over her had ceased on her last birthday. She was truly an independent woman, and if maintaining that status meant forgoing the romantic love she portrayed with such heartrending reality on the stage, it was a sacrifice she was more than willing to make.

In any event Stacia was only too well aware that there were few choices open to her. Marriage options were few to actresses, who were considered no better than bits of muslin by the gentlemen who pursued them with such assiduousness. Most actresses sought and hoped for the protection of men of the town like Lord Silverwood. Becoming a left-handed wife to a gentleman of means was the summit of most actresses' ambition. Smiling grimly, Stacia thought she would prefer marriage to Erasmus Chark.

"I live in fear the audience will one day find me out as a sham," she told her mentor as he stood beaming at her in the doorway.

Ormerod Greaves frowned. "A sham you are not, my love, but I do feel your talent lies in drawing from experience. It comes from deep within you.

68

That much has always been evident to me. You have known the despair you portray so eloquently onstage."

Stacia couldn't gainsay him on that score, and a moment later he declared, "I must go now and check on our receipts for the evening. We'll meet later for supper as usual and discuss the performance in more detail."

He swept out of the doorway, slamming the door closed behind him. As she sat down at the dressing table and began to remove her heavy stage makeup, Maura went to pack away the gowns Stacia had worn throughout the evening's performance.

"It's good that Mr. Greaves acknowledges who keeps this company up in the stirrups nowadays," she said, "even if Mrs. Sanbourne does not."

"She may have an excess of pride," Stacia replied, "but even she is more accepting than she used to be."

"Marietta Sanbourne is a fly lady who has, like the rest of us, grown accustomed to an easier life of late."

Stacia turned back to the mirror and reflected how right Ormerod had been in his assessment of her ability. When hatred was called upon, all she needed to do was conjure up the well-remembered recollection of Lord Silverwood. When despair was the emotion needed, she recalled the time she was obliged to leave Dover's End for her uncle's house, never to return. Of love she had no experience, save a faint memory of her parents' happiness before the death of her mother changed everything, but there were feelings she was able to conjure up when she was called upon to act out a great passion, although she didn't care to examine too closely how she was able to portray it so well. Perhaps, she mused, she was a greater actress than anyone acknowledged, or it might well be that the passion of love was not so dissimilar to that of hatred. It was something she didn't care to think about too closely.

Stacia had changed out of her outlandish stage clothes, stowed her wig, and was just about to tie the strings of her new spring bonnet when a knock at the door heralded a visitor. The man was a stranger, as were most of her admirers. Even her most ardent followers were reluctant to do more than pay a brief tribute to her, and in any event she always moved on at the end of the week.

This visitor was a nondescript type of man, but one who reeked of sophistication. He exhibited none of the diffidence she was accustomed to in those who were in awe of her as an actress.

"Miss Gilbert?"

"Yes?"

"My name is Thomas Allbury. . . ."

He spoke in a manner to indicate she might know him, and momentarily she froze with fear, thinking he must be a Bow Street runner engaged by her uncle to track her down. But then she relaxed a little. Uncle Quentin would never pay someone to find her. There was no reason, especially now she was of age.

He handed her an engraved card, which she took hesitantly. "I'm the manager of the Regency Theatre in London."

Stacia smiled at last as she fingered his card, feeling foolish for her alarm. Unfortunately being wary had become something of a habit since her flight from Brackentree.

70

"Mr. Allbury, how kind of you to call in."

At the other side of the room Stacia was aware of Maura standing stiffly, her pose expectant. Stacia suspected she was also holding her breath.

"I was most impressed with your performance this evening, Miss Gilbert. The gentleman sitting next to me was most affected."

"I'm obliged to you, sir, for saying so."

All the while he spoke, Thomas Allbury was scrutinizing Stacia in a most discomfiting manner. Suddenly he smiled. "Miss Gilbert, I must cut line here. I am here expressly to offer you an engagement at the Regency."

Stacia gasped, and Maura made some kind of similar sound. "That's wonderful," the woman said when Stacia made no response.

"Does the prospect appeal to you?" the man asked.

Finally, glancing helplessly at her friend, Stacia found her voice. "You may be certain it does, sir. However, I couldn't accept—much as I am grateful to you for what is obviously a very great honor, I cannot possibly leave the company."

"Stacia!" Maura said in a warning tone.

"I appreciate your loyalty, ma'am, but I have already discussed the matter with Mr. Greaves, and he is willing, for a consideration from me, to release you."

"He is?" Stacia asked in amazement. She was both heartened and disappointed at the same time.

"You need not make an immediate decision," Mr. Allbury told her. "You must think on it, and it might be best if you were to discuss the matter with Mr. Greaves before any final decision is made."

As he spoke, Stacia toyed nervously with the ribbon of her reticule. "I would appreciate your indulgence in the matter, sir."

"With your permission, ma'am, I propose to call upon you on the morrow at your lodgings, after breakfast perhaps?"

She nodded, and after he had taken his leave of them, she turned to Maura, crying, "London! The Regency! I cannot conceive of this. If only it were possible."

"Tush! Of course it is possible. There is no question about it. You must go, and there's an end to it."

"How can I? Naturally Ormerod is being characteristically generous in letting me go, but I cannot allow him to make such a sacrifice on my behalf. What would happen to the troupe if I did?"

"Listen to me, Stacia," Maura said, gripping her by both arms and shaking her gently, "you must take this offer. It might never happen again."

Tears sprang to Stacia's eyes. "Oh, Maura, how can I go and leave you all?"

"Don't delude yourself, girl. If the offer was made to Mrs. Sanbourne or Mr. Greaves, or indeed any one of us, we would go in a brace of snaps with no thought for anyone else."

Stacia suspected as much herself, but she did feel she owed so much to her mentor, she could not possibly abandon him now. However, when she arrived at their lodgings for supper, Ormerod Greaves greeted her warmly, clasping both her hands in his. He appeared as excited at the new development as Stacia herself.

"True success at last, my dear! I am so proud of you! We all are!"

She stole a glance at Marietta Sanbourne, who, even more surprisingly, looked benign. "My success of late has sufficed for me, Mr. Greaves. I owe it in full measure to the example you have both shown me."

The actor clucked his tongue. "Stuff and nonsense, child. A chance of an engagement in London is not to be passed by. It is time for you to move on. You have a talent beyond that required for traveling actors, a style reminiscent of the great Peg Woffington. A London engagement is what we all hope for, and I suspected an offer to you was only a matter of time."

"You tell her she must go," Maura insisted. "An offer like this might never come again."

Stacia clasped Ormerod's bearlike hands in her own small ones as if she was afraid to let them go. "I cannot leave you. Any of you! You're like my family. You *are* my family."

"You left your family once, did you not?" Mrs. Sanbourne pointed out. "You can do so again now that success is beckoning."

"That was different. I was unhappy then, but I've been happy traveling with all of you."

Marietta Sanbourne came up to them then, saying, "If you do not go, you will forever regret missing this opportunity."

"Mrs. Sanbourne, I . . ."

As she spoke, Marietta slipped her arm into that of Ormerod Greaves and looked up at him. "If it helps you determine what to do, I feel I should tell you that Ormerod and I have decided to retire. We're getting too old for traveling, if truth be told.

Mr. Allbury has promised to stage a benefit in our honor, and that should be most useful to our plans." She paused and looked almost bashful before she added, "Ormerod has honored me with an offer of marriage, and I fully intend to accept."

"How wonderful!" Stacia cried after a moment's astonished pause, and Maura added, "We wish you both happiness, truly we do."

"So you see," Mr. Greaves pointed out, "you can leave us with no regrets."

Marietta Sanbourne looked up at her husband-to-be again before continuing, "We've had a long-held wish to settle in Brighton, ever since we played *Othello* there to great acclaim. Perhaps we'll start a little theater there in due course. Billy will come with us, and we'll make our home together for the very first time. You must go to London, Stacia. You are better than you know. Take the opportunity that never came my way. You are a better actress than I ever was."

Stacia's throat constricted with emotion. She turned to Maura, who was smiling at her encouragingly, and said a moment later, "I will accept Mr. Allbury's offer only if he agrees to allow Maura to accompany me as my dresser."

When the woman began to protest, "You mustn't compromise your chance—" Stacia added in a tone that broached no argument, "You may be sure I shall insist upon it."

A few moments later they were all embracing with tears flowing freely until Ormerod extricated himself, sniffing loudly and saying, "I believe we should celebrate this new adventure we are all about to embark upon with champagne, my dears. Now that Sarah Siddons has retired, we must drink a toast to her successor—Miss Stacia Gilbert!"

SEVEN

Reports of the new actress's debut spread throughout the theatergoing public in London as soon as her initial season was announced. As was usual in such matters, her prowess was exaggerated until she was attributed almost mythical abilities.

This knowledge added to the total of Stacia's nervousness as she prepared for her first performance at the Regency Theatre. Fortunately, she was not going to be obliged to play an unfamiliar role; Mr. Allbury had decided that her debut performance should be in *The Devilish Earl*, so impressed had he been with her acting in the part of the heroine. Her acting partner was to be Paris Kingswell, a young actor who had already played two seasons at the Regency to great acclaim. Unlike the other great actors, Kean and Kemble, Paris Kingswell possessed a handsome countenance as well as a remarkable talent. Mr. Allbury was convinced that their partnership of good looks as well as acting ability would go well with the patrons of the theater.

"The newspapers are already calling you the new Kembles," Maura told her as she fitted on Stacia's beautiful new costume.

The wigs and gowns provided were of the finest quality, and Stacia was given a comfortable dressing room to occupy at last. When she first came to London, she'd taken lodgings in a fine house in Tavistock Square, not too far from the theater, but a pleasant area still occupied in great part by members of the ton.

"Do not, I beg of you, make me more nervous than I already am," Stacia begged as she ran her fingers down the smooth satin of her skirt and inspected her reflection critically in the mirror.

Maura simply laughed, having grown used over the years to Stacia's diffidence. "Just pretend you're in one of the provincial theaters we know so well."

"But it isn't! This is London, and the audience is so sophisticated."

"The play's the same. Just act as well as you usually do and you will be wonderful."

"You are a dear to say so, but we're not playing for rustics, Maura. The people out there are discerning theatergoers, critics of Kemble, Mrs. Jordan, and all the great actors of our time. How can I possibly live up to such competition?"

"Tush! Try not to be so blue-deviled. You have yet to be booed off the stage."

"There is always a first time!"

"My dear, you mustn't doubt yourself. This could be your most triumphant engagement."

"I shall be glad when this evening is over, but at least we can forget about drafty dressing rooms and dusty theaters, although if my performance tonight doesn't exceed expectations, I'm afraid we might be obliged to endure those privations again!"

"Don't dare to make mention of such a possibility!" Maura begged as she tidied a few hairs in Stacia's wig. "I'm just growing nicely accustomed to

77

aired sheets and good, hot food, not to mention the shops in Oxford Street and Bond Street. Did you ever see such an array of gewgaws to buy? Now if only we possessed the money to purchase some of them . . ."

Stacia got to her feet, smoothing out her gown with a nervous hand. "If I am a success tonight, we should, before long, be able to afford to shop with the finest. Even before I've appeared, tradesmen are offering me credit."

"That is the way of the fashionables," Maura told her.

"It is not my way. I still retain clear memories of the creditors dunning Papa at regular intervals. Soon we shall be sufficiently well breeched not to require credit, and we'll go shopping every day if we wish!"

"Indeed," Maura answered with a laugh. "Now you're being positive, which is all I hoped for. All you need for success is to be seen by the critics."

"Critics, Maura! My goodness, they'll be out there too tonight. I wish you had not reminded me!"

"They will adore you, be certain."

Mr. Allbury popped his head round the door, smiled, and said, "Ravishing, my dear," before rushing off.

Only a moment later Paris Kingswell appeared. He was flushed beneath his makeup. "The start is put back a few minutes. Did you know?"

"No one has told me," Stacia responded breathlessly. "What is amiss, Paris?"

"Nothing. Nothing!" It was evident he could scarcely contain his excitement. "It is just that there is such a squeeze in Tottenham Court Road, with landaus and carriages and the like trying to

78

reach the theater, many of the patrons are bound to be late. Allbury keeps checking the box office, but there's not a seat to be had, and that's with Kemble appearing at Covent Garden and Kean at Drury Lane!"

So saying, he rushed off to spread the glad tidings to other members of the company.

Stacia clasped one hand to her lips and began to laugh nervously. "Oh, my goodness. This is like to be the night of my triumph or the greatest boner of my life!"

As Stacia, in her role of Dorabella, sank down onto the boards in the final death scene, an acting feat she had come to perform so well, there was a hush in every part of the auditorium. After her first few minutes onstage, she had known instinctively that the audience was with her, and so great was her feeling of triumph, it was difficult then to continue playing the utter despair the role called for.

The moment the curtain fell, the audience erupted into applause, and as she took countless calls, Stacia couldn't help but bask in the triumph of the moment. Uncle Quentin and his cheeseparing charity were truly consigned to the past. Her success meant not only a full theater whenever she was billed to appear but also financial security, so, she reflected gleefully, when she was finally allowed off the stage, the future couldn't fail to be brilliant.

While she rushed away to her dressing room to rest and prepare for her appearance in the second half, a much lighter fare to raise the spirits of those dejected by the tragedy that had gone before, many of those in the theater rose to take a turn about the lobby and find refreshment at one of the bars, but the talk was an excited one of the performance they'd all enjoyed.

A bright new talent had arrived on the London stage, and those privileged to witness her debut were anxious to talk about it, especially on the morrow to those unfortunates who had not been able to obtain tickets.

Unknown to Stacia, one member of the audience sat poker-faced in his private box, unmoved by the general excitement going on all around him. Although all the other boxes were crammed to capacity, he shared his only with his wife.

"Well, Peg," Damian Farramond told her, "my suspicion has proved well founded after all. My sister is the one all the talk has been about of late. For all these years she's been living the amoral life of an *actress*."

The last word was almost spat out in disgust, and his wife, equally grim-faced, told him, "I'd liefer she'd become a Covent Garden nun than this."

"Either way could mean social disaster for us."

"Only last week I heard an on-dit about her. It's rumored she's been living . . ." Peggy Farramond paused to dab delicately at her lips with a lace-edged handkerchief, and her husband glanced at her anxiously.

"Yes, Peggy, what is it you heard?"

"I heard . . ." Mrs. Farramond looked pale even in the dim light of the theater. "I heard she'd been the doxy of the company manager." When she turned to look at him, her face was a picture of misery. "What are we to do, Damian?"

"There is little we can do. Even at a tender age Eustacia was always disobliging. She's of age now

80

and will do exactly as she pleases, just as she used to do."

"Oh . . ."

"It is at least fortunate she has had the good sense to adopt our mother's maiden name, although I am in no way pleased she has chosen to use it in this manner, but at least it will mean no person of respectability—no member of the ton—will associate her with us."

"There must be something we can do to stop her, Damian! She cannot be allowed to ruin our life in the beau monde just when we are being accepted. Lady Dewsbury is taking me up! If she knew about . . . Oh, it is not to be borne."

"She cannot ruin anything for us, Peg."

"How can you say so? Do you realize how great my humiliation is like to be if the tattle-baskets discover she is your sister? *An actress!*"

"I tell you there is naught I can do save appeal to her better nature, and that will be to no avail, I assure you."

"Then you must offer her something to make her stop. Anything!"

"I can only reiterate it will be to no avail. I am as out of countenance as you."

"What if she makes the connection known to all and sundry?"

"She will not, my dear. I have no intention of making myself known to her, and she can have no notion we have taken up residence in London. Even if she did, my sister possesses a good deal of the Farramond pride, and she will not claim a connection if we do not. In any event I cast her off years ago. She is nothing to my family now. We must seek to protect our reputation and that of our children."

"She acted well, I must own, even though the play was a trifle melodramatic for my liking. The audience received it well."

"That is a great misfortune." Her husband sighed. "It means it is unlike she will return to wherever she has been hiding these past five years." He pushed back his chair, adding, "I believe we have seen enough of this nonsense, my dear. Let us be gone from here with no further delay."

"An actress, Damian," Peggy said despairingly. "How could she do that to us? We have never sought to harm *her*."

While the Farramonds discussed their calamitous discovery, in a box nearby quite a different conversation was taking place.

"Damn!" Sir Hubert Patch exclaimed. "I remember that chit from some rustic theater, although I'll go bale if I can remember where it was."

"Dorrington," Lord Silverwood supplied, having viewed the preceding drama with no perceivable emotion apparent. "It was Dorrington."

"My stars! So it was! It was the weekend Blatcher fought MacGuire, and I lost a pony. Your memory is excellent, Sil."

"Indeed it is," his lordship replied darkly.

"Fetching chit, as I recall," Sir Hubert went on, despite the earl's obvious displeasure. "Quite took your fancy, if I am not mistaken." When Lord Silverwood didn't deign to reply, he added, "She might have been fetching then, but she's become quite a beauty since. That can't have escaped your notice. You might find more favor with her now, my friend."

82

"I have no intention of currying favor with her, Hu," the earl replied.

Although he had watched the play and admired the acting, the memory of being dismissed so coldly by such a green girl had returned to taunt him.

"No mercy, eh, Sil? How like you that is. Never mind. Miss Gilbert won't lack for attention now she's here in town, and I daresay you're well enough occupied with your little Italian songbird."

The earl smiled at last. "Indeed I am."

"I can't blame that in you. You beat a good deal of competition for her favors, not that I doubted you would." Suddenly Sir Hubert looked thoughtful. "All the same, if the field's clear, I might make myself known to this bit of muslin. Send her a gewgaw or two. That might find favor with her."

"You're very welcome, sir," was his friend's tart rejoinder. "You even have my blessing."

Sir Hubert cast his friend a sly look. "By gad! You *were* taken with her! I wish I'd had a wager on the possibility of Blaise Silverwood being given the go-by by an actress, no less."

"That she was disobliging remains her misfortune, not mine."

"I don't doubt the Italian songbird is far more obliging."

Lord Silverwood leaned forward and affected an air of confidentiality. "Let us hope you find Miss Gilbert equally accommodating, Hu. If so, you will discover yourself as merry as a grig."

Sir Hubert roared with laughter as Lady Charlotte Fitch-Drummond came into the box. "Such laughter, gentlemen," she chided. "How can you be so happy after watching Miss Gilbert's acting? I declare I am still sorely affected by it."

"Your brother, ma'am, was not moved in the slightest," Sir Hubert answered maliciously, "at least not on this occasion, so he tells me."

"The only role I'd like to see Miss Gilbert portray in the future," the earl declared in his driest manner, "is that of Katherine in *The Taming of the Shrew*."

His sister's eyebrows quirked upward. "Such spleen, my dear, and so unwarranted."

Lady Charlotte was an accredited beauty, and on her marriage to the ineffectual but exceedingly wealthy Ashley Fitch-Drummond she had become one of the leading hostesses of the ton. Known for her vivacity and charm, like many members of the Silverwood clan, she now exuded an air of excitement about her.

"I have, gentlemen, achieved a considerable coup this evening, and you are the first to know of it," she told them as she retained her seat and began to fan herself.

"How like you, my lady," Sir Hubert replied, "although I cannot conceive what it is that is out of the ordinary, for you are accustomed to achieving marvels."

Lady Charlotte smiled at his flattery before confiding, "I have succeeded in engaging Miss Gilbert's presence at my soiree next week."

"My stars!" Sir Hubert exclaimed. "My lady, you are a marvel. Miss Gilbert is certainly up to the knocker, so your soiree is guaranteed to be a pink night."

Once again the lady smiled at the baronet before continuing to explain, "She has agreed to attend, and so has Mr. Kingswell. They will make some

84

readings. I don't mind confessing, my dears, I am in high snuff at the achievement."

"And so you should be!" Sir Hubert assured her.

Lord Silverwood had been regarding his sister indulgently, but now he said, affecting an air of fashionable boredom, "Not another bluestocking event, Lottie."

"Indeed not. Miss Gilbert will now be all the crack, unless I am very much mistaken. *Everyone* will wish to hear her recitation and make her acquaintance. I am delighted it will be at my soiree!"

"We look forward to it with relish," Sir Hubert told her, at the same time glancing maliciously at his friend. "I am persuaded your brother is in a fidge to make her acquaintance."

The earl merely smiled with faint irony as his sister answered tartly, "If he has aspirations in that direction, Sir Hubert, he is bound for a disappointment, for Miss Gilbert does not appear to me to be the kind of actress Blaise usually pursues with determination."

"I am not obliged to pursue every actress who appears on the London stage," her brother reminded her.

"Obliged to, no, but inclined—yes. Even so, you would not find her in the least responsive, I fancy. Despite her obvious beauty and considerable talent, she appears rather self-effacing, rather like Mrs. Siddons, I imagine."

"But rather more handsome," Sir Hubert pointed out.

"Equally virtuous was the point I was trying to make," Lady Charlotte scolded. "She exudes an air of propriety Blaise would not in the least appreciate."

Sir Hubert chuckled. "I fear, my lady, all this talk will merely encourage him."

Lord Silverwood had been tapping the balustrade in his boredom. Now he drew a sigh and got to his feet. "By your leave, Lottie, Hu, I find this unstinting praise of Miss Gilbert utterly tedious."

"You are so easily bored," his sister chided.

"I am in the face of normally sensible ladies and gentlemen who become unhinged when confronted with some bread-and-butter miss feigning the most elementary histrionics."

"Oh, dear," Lady Charlotte lamented when her brother had gone. "I fancy he has gone to greet that boxful of cyprians who have been ogling him disgustingly all through the play."

"I have the feeling Miss Gilbert's becoming all the crack will not in the least be agreeable to your brother, my dear."

Lady Charlotte looked only mildly surprised. "I cannot conceive why the matter would be of the least interest to him—and while we are speaking of such matters, I feel it incumbent upon me to say that because you are a good friend of his, I do wish you would encourage him at least to acknowledge some of the heiresses who throw themselves at his head every Season, Sir Hubert. If the Silverwood title dies out with my brother, I shall appoint you with a large portion of the blame."

"I must protest at such an unjust accusation, my lady. There is no possible use in blaming me for your brother's omissions. His duty to his family is self-evident. No one is more aware of it than Blaise, but he can be contrary."

"Oh, indeed," Lady Charlotte replied with a small groan.

"Moreover, he has been thoroughly spoiled by females throwing the handkerchief."

"On occasions some of them throw even more than that!"

Sir Hubert smiled. "No one throws themselves at my head, so I have no experience of it, and in any event Silverwood never listens to me on any score."

"He never listens to anyone," Lady Charlotte lamented as the curtain began to rise, and an expectant hush descended upon the audience once again.

EIGHT

"Just listen to this, Stacia!" Mr. Allbury cried, unable to contain his excitement as he read through the most important journals and magazines.

He was pacing up and down Stacia's neat drawing room, while she sat with a new play in her lap and Maura was ensconced on the window seat, sewing. The room was somewhat overwhelmed with some of the flowers she had received, and the atmosphere was pervaded by their sickly perfume.

"Palatinus in the *Gentleman's Magazine* is quite favorable, even though restrained, but he is rarely enthusiastic over anyone. He says, 'Miss Gilbert is the newest star in London's theater firmament. Although we have not seen her perform many roles, her portrayal in *The Devilish Earl* undoubtedly is a fine one, and it will be interesting to chart her progress when she tackles other parts of high caliber.'"

He looked up from the journal. "You must understand, Palatinus is not usually generous with his praise."

"I am truly honored, sir."

Mr. Allbury flapped the journal in the air in a gesture of impatience. "I have witnessed actresses succumb to the vapors for far less praise than this, madam."

Stacia remained serene. "It is indeed exciting, Mr. Allbury, and I am most grateful to the gentleman for his praise, but this success has come so swiftly, I scarce dare acknowledge it as yet for fear it will disappear and Maura and I will discover ourselves back in some dingy, dirty barn, performing for disinterested rustics."

Thomas Allbury flung himself into the chair nearest to her. "That will never happen now, my dear. You are made. You have taken. You are all the crack! You must know it from those who fight to acknowledge you, some of the most fashionable and sophisticated people in town! I knew you would take from the moment I saw you perform in Manchester. You can have no comprehension how rare a find you are. Sometimes I search for years for a new talent to bring to the Regency. . . ."

"We live in a fickle world. What is fashionable today may not be all the crack on the morrow."

Mr. Allbury clucked his tongue. "What makes you so Friday-faced? Most actresses of my acquaintance cry roast meat at the first vapid compliment." He turned to Maura and asked, "Why this attack of the dismals, Mrs. Copeland? I look to you for some explanation, for I cannot find one, in all conscience."

Maura looked similarly mystified, and Stacia hastened to explain to them, "I am truly delighted with my reception, sir, and I assure you I am not in the least blue-deviled, but I do happen to know how it is possible for good fortune and wealth to disappear overnight."

"Very well. If you persist in being downish, let us

proceed further nevertheless. I propose our next major presentation to be *Jane Shore*."

"*Jane Shore!*" Stacia exclaimed.

Mr. Allbury frowned. "Yes, do you have any objection to that?"

"Only in respect of it being a most difficult role to play, sir."

"That is of no account. You are equal to it, in my opinion."

"My goodness, do you not recall that Mrs. Siddons played it successfully on many occasions during her career?"

"So will you if you have a mind to," Maura pointed out.

"I have no mind to invite comparisons."

"You are already being compared with her," Maura confided, "and favorably, too."

"That is frightening," Stacia responded, "but the greatest honor, I must own."

"I have considered *Venice Preserved*, if you prefer," Mr. Allbury offered, something that made Stacia laugh.

"What a choice you offer me, sir—to die by starvation or go slowly mad."

"I considered those particular plays only because I deemed them ideally suited to your talents for tragedy, my dear. You play such roles to perfection. Indeed you are being referred to in fashionable circles as the Tragedy Queen, which is a great honor."

Stacia was certainly aware of the title, which amused her. "You must make the final decision, and I will certainly abide by it," she told Mr. Allbury.

"I am persuaded you will succeed very well in either role, but I will think on it and perhaps consult Mr. Kingswell to solicit his preference." He paused before he went on, "It is splendid that you will do a reading at Lady Charlotte Fitch-Drummond's soiree."

Stacia drew a sigh at the reminder, which was not a welcome one. "That was not my choice. Maura accepted on my behalf before I had any chance to refuse."

"Only because I knew you *would* refuse."

"Why should you wish to refuse?" Mr. Allbury demanded to know, looking from one lady to the other in some confusion. "Lady Charlotte is top of the trees in this town, I assure you. If she condescends to take you up, it will be the greatest honor. You cannot afford to offend members of the beau monde, my dear."

"I had no notion to offend her ladyship, Mr. Allbury, only—"

"Lady Charlotte has excellent connections, apart from an uncle who, I believe, died penniless of drink some years ago, but that is of no account."

Stacia laughed harshly. "That is not an uncommon fate, sir, I assure you!"

"This invitation could not be better timed. You will be mingling in very elevated company, my dear. I truly cannot think why you should wish to decline her invitation. I am indebted to Mrs. Copeland for being needle-witted enough to accept on your behalf."

"As I have intimated, it is merely that I am unused to all the attention I am receiving," Stacia explained, but it sounded lame to her own ears.

"The attention you are receiving will only intensify as your fame grows. Only the other evening I espied Arnold, from Drury Lane, in the audience. He may only have been spying out the competition—something we all do from time to time—but I warned him to desist if he had any designs upon you." His eyes narrowed. "He has not sought you out, has he, my dear?"

"No, and if he does, I will be sure to send him away with a flea in his ear."

"That's the barber! It is a considerable relief to me to hear you say so. After all, it was I who discovered you."

"I am fully appreciative of that, sir. I wouldn't leave the Regency whatever the inducements put before me."

Mr. Allbury seemed satisfied as he got to his feet. "You are most uncommon, Miss Gilbert, I am bound to own."

When he reached the door, he turned to look at her consideringly for a moment or two before saying, "I believe we will try you in comedy very soon."

Stacia brightened immediately. "I should like that exceedingly well, sir. Meanwhile I shall read both *Venice Preserved* and *Jane Shore*."

"Just at present it might be a good notion for you to take some air," Mr. Allbury suggested as he prepared to leave. He subjected her to a searching look. "You appear pale, my dear, and that is becoming only in a dying heroine. Take Mrs. Copeland for a stroll in Hyde Park. Do the grand strut. It will do you both good."

When he had gone, Stacia said, "I never looked for all the acclaim I'm receiving, Maura. I just wanted to keep out of my uncle's clutches until I came of age. It is ironic I have achieved all this success, is it not?"

Maura smiled kindly. "It is when you consider that someone like Mrs. Sanbourne tried for most of her life to reach your position. You no longer have anything to fear from your uncle." After a moment she ventured, "Why do we not heed Mr. Allbury's advice and take a turn in the park? It is a fine day, and I should certainly appreciate the air."

Stacia turned away. "I think not. It would be difficult to enjoy such an outing with people wishing to accost me at every step, and all those bucks vying for my favor."

"It would be any young lady's dream to be in such a position," Maura pointed out.

"Yes, if they were in earnest, I agree it would be so, but what they want of me I am not willing to give."

"I wonder if the root of your reluctance has more to do with a fear of encountering one specific gentleman rather than the large number who merely admire your talent."

Stacia smiled faintly and answered, "I have a better notion. Let us go instead to Oxford Street and purchase some ribbons. That, I think, will be an altogether more enjoyable experience for us both. We might even purchase some material for new gowns! Do you think that would be totally extravagant of us?"

Maura shook her head wryly and went to fetch her bonnet and pelisse while Stacia called for the carriage Mr. Allbury had put at their disposal.

The two ladies emerged from the haberdasher's emporium chattering excitedly. As they might have expected, their attempt to purchase buttons and ribbons to match the materials they had bought was constantly thwarted by those who wished to felicitate Stacia on her acting. She graciously accepted all the praise offered to her, but it took them much longer than anticipated to complete their purchases.

"I fancy actresses and the like are obliged to employ others to make their purchases for them," Maura ventured laughingly as they eventually emerged into the street.

"Not if they have spent years without the means to make the most elementary purchases," Stacia retorted. "In those circumstances they enjoy it exceedingly well, despite all the interruptions."

Maura chuckled. "Did you note how the proprietor greased your boots? I thought he was like to hit his forehead on the ground, so low did he bow!"

Stacia laughed delightedly. "It is quite a novelty for me to be assailed by toadies, I assure you, but one to which I could soon grow accustomed."

"You deserve your success, none more so."

Momentarily Stacia was downcast. "If my mother were alive, she would be horrified that I have become an actress. She was a Gilbert of Driffield, but the family cast her off when she married my father."

Maura frowned slightly. "I always understood that your father's family was most respectable."

"They are, but Grandfather Gilbert was a lord lieutenant of North Yorkshire, and Papa was a scapegrace even then, albeit a charming one."

"If your mother had been alive today, I daresay you'd be safely buckled to some worthy young man by now. You might even have a brood of children to occupy you."

Wryly Stacia replied, "No doubt, and I daresay I would be most content with my situation in life."

She glanced expectantly to where they had left the carriage. Their driver was in conversation with another and had not seen them, and just as Stacia raised her gloved hand to attract his attention, she caught sight of a high-perch phaeton coming down the road from the direction of Tyburn Corner.

Her hand wavered in the air as she paused to admire the phaeton, which was lacquered in black with a gold escutcheon painted on the door. Stacia racked her mind for the long-forgotten Latin she had learned sitting in on Damian's lessons with his tutor. *Glory to the Valiant*, she quickly translated the motto. The carriage was drawn by a matched team of coal black horses. She knew enough about cattle to recognize these were fine bloods, possibly the best Tattersall's had to offer.

She had scarce begun to admire them when she became aware of the driver on the box. He was wearing a high-crowned beaver and a drab greatcoat fastened by brass buttons. When he caught sight of her standing on the curbside, he began to pull in, causing Stacia to stiffen with outrage. Almost immediately she was tempted to shrink back, but pride forbade her to do so. She remained at the curbside, her face set into an expression of the most utter distaste.

The driver raised his hat and stared down at her, and she knew he couldn't help but be aware of her feelings for him, so plain were they to see on her countenance. His height, compared to hers, meant he always looked down on her, and from his lofty perch on the box of the phaeton she felt more intimidated than ever. Then he smiled, an ironic smile that filled her heart with hatred anew, causing her to glance around briefly for a means of escape. It seemed her life was meant to be tormented by this man, and there was precious little she could do about it.

"Why, it's Miss Gilbert, is it not?"

"I think you know very well who I am, Lord Silverwood."

One dark eyebrow quirked upward in the manner she recalled all too well. "As it was several years ago that our paths crossed briefly and you have encountered considerable success since, your memory is as good as your talent for memorizing lines, ma'am."

"I could scarce forget *you*, my lord," she responded, and her bitterness was naturally lost on him.

His scrutiny of her was as thorough as on that last occasion, and even though she was now wearing a pelisse over her gown, she felt his inspection as keenly as she had at that time. His own thoughts must have been dwelling on similar lines, for he smiled roguishly and said, "You are wearing rather more clothes than on the last time I had occasion to clap eyes upon you."

Her cheeks grew pink at the verbal reminder, which was totally unnecessary. "It is most unchivalrous of you to make mention of it, and as *I* recall, you burst into my dressing room uninvited."

The smile faded abruptly. "Ah, yes, it was uncouth of me, I confess. Belated apologies are called for, ma'am, and I bestow them upon you unreservedly." As Stacia fumed at what she knew to be his sarcasm, he added, "I would have been somewhat more circumspect had I known you would one day become the toast of the town, and even more aware, I fancy, of your own consequence than you were when you languished unknown in shabby provincial theaters."

He nodded briefly and unsmilingly to both ladies, and then, flicking his whip over the back of the leader of his team, he drove away.

"What an utterly horrid man!" Stacia gasped.

Maura looked rueful as their own carriage rumbled to a halt and the footman started to pull down the steps. "It is certain he has a knack of setting up your bristles, but I cannot conceive why you took him in such dislike from the outset."

"It was evident to me on our first encounter he was a fribble," Stacia answered dismissively as she frowned at the swiftly departing phaeton.

"I have it in mind you had incredible foresight on that first brief meeting," Maura persisted. "I think him rather charming."

"I did not solicit your opinion," Stacia told her with uncharacteristic sharpness as she sank back into the well-sprung carriage.

"I do wonder if your encounter with his lordship in Dorrington was your first," Maura mused, unfazed by Stacia's sharpness. "I fancy you and he might have met before. You were so comfortable with your dislike of him."

Stacia didn't answer. As the carriage set off back to Tavistock Square, her thoughts were dark ones.

London was a large city by any comparison, but when Lord Silverwood was also in residence, it certainly wasn't big enough to accommodate the both of them.

NINE

"Appearing at Lady Charlotte's soiree is making me as nervous as any night in the theater I can ever recall," Stacia confessed as they made their way to the Fitch-Drummond mansion in Piccadilly.

Both ladies were wearing new gowns, Stacia's of jonquil silk decorated with pearls. Her burnished curls were swept up into a classic chignon, and a fillet that matched her gown kept them in order.

"Just look upon it as another performance," Maura suggested.

"You are always so full of good sense, Maura. I really don't know what I would do without you."

Maura flushed with pleasure at the compliment. "You would do well enough."

"I don't suppose I need to concern myself too much about being well received," Stacia reasoned. "I feel my rep is made, and one reading cannot tarnish it."

"You are becoming easier with your fame," her companion pointed out.

"After the years of deprivation, I fully intend to enjoy what fame has to offer me."

"As long as it is not Lord Silverwood," Maura pointed out mischievously.

"Nor any gentleman of a rakish disposition."

When the carriage drew up outside the imposing

facade of Lady Charlotte's mansion, Maura said as she glanced out of the window, "We shall certainly be elevating ourselves this evening. Lady Charlotte is haut ton."

Stacia's previously ebullient spirits sank a little at the reminder. Maura's mention of Lord Silverwood was a sobering one, and Stacia fervently hoped that this particular member of the beau monde would not be present this evening. She hadn't considered that unpleasant possibility up until now, for she presumed him more likely to haunt gambling hells rather than soirees where recitations of poetry were the principal diversion.

The Fitch-Drummonds' house was packed with people by the time the two ladies arrived, for Stacia was obliged to appear at the Regency first and had agreed to attend the soiree only after the performance. Lady Charlotte's house steward escorted her up the stairs, and by the time she reached the top, Stacia felt much more relaxed, for everyone she encountered greeted her warmly.

"They are not in the least stiff-rumped," Maura whispered.

"No indeed," Stacia agreed. "Everyone is most condescending."

Maura glanced around her in awe. "Is this not the most splendid house? I wonder how many rooms there are. I have never seen the like."

"Nor I, but I'm told there are finer, and even larger, houses to be seen."

"I don't believe a word of it."

Lady Charlotte came to greet them in the warmest of tones. "Everyone is in a fidge to hear you recite, Miss Gilbert."

In truth Stacia was almost overwhelmed by the

number of people present. She had understood a soiree to be something like the ones her parents used to hold, a very small gathering of close acquaintances. The mansion was packed to capacity, and guests spilled out of every room they passed and into the corridors and hallways. There were sufficient candles alight to empty a country chandler's shop.

"Mr. Kingswell has already arrived," Lady Charlotte told her, "so the evening promises to be a splendid one. We truly are most grateful to you for being here."

"The pleasure is mine," Stacia murmured, glancing around and exhibiting more unease than was warranted.

It had been agreed earlier with Lady Charlotte that Stacia would read from the current literary sensation *Childe Harold's Pilgrimage*, and when she had finished to great applause from the appreciative audience, she was astounded to receive approval of her rendition from the author himself. Lord Byron limped up to her and was unsparing in his praise of her rendition of his masterpiece.

Meanwhile some of the guests had hurried away to the card room to resume gaming while others awaited the call to supper as the ballroom was made ready for dancing. The knowledge that hardened gamesters had abandoned their cards and dice to hear her recitation was an indication of their regard for her talent, and Stacia was moved to realize it.

While Stacia received the praise of Lady Charlotte's guests, the lady herself espied her brother from across the room and made her way toward him. "Blaise, I didn't look to see you here. As I recall, you declared your intention of crying off this particular diversion."

He smiled ruefully. "I know changing one's mind is considered a lady's prerogative, but I am claiming it as mine on this occasion."

Her face relaxed into a welcoming smile. "As always I am delighted to see you, and I am not alone in my pleasure. That little Miss Seymour was asking of you earlier, and her disappointment when I informed her you were elsewhere was most affecting. She is a pretty little thing, you know, as well as being bang up to the mark."

The earl made much of adjusting his already perfectly set cuffs. "I had almost forgotten why I normally cry off your squeezes, Lottie," he answered dryly. "You must have realized by now, my dear, Miss Seymour is not in the least to my taste."

"I am in despair of finding anyone who is— someone who is welcome in polite society, that is. There are other debutantes, you know—many of them—who ask after you."

"How obliging of them," he answered, with a lack of enthusiasm that made his sister sigh.

"Miss Gilbert recited well, did she not?" he asked in a deliberate effort to change the subject from that of his continuing bachelorhood.

Immediately Lady Charlotte brightened. "I'm so glad you arrived in time to hear her recitation, Blaise. We all enjoyed it. Everyone could hear every word perfectly, even in this crowded room, and yet she speaks in normal circumstances so softly. Would you care for me to introduce you to her?"

"No need," he said hastily, and then, glancing beyond her shoulder, said, "I see Dec Whitney and must have words with him."

Lady Charlotte looked wistful as she watched him go, and then she went on to talk to more of her guests.

After remaining surrounded for some considerable time by those who would have words with her, Stacia felt she needed to take some air, and as she had lost sight of Maura some time ago, she wandered out of the ballroom and into the welcoming cool of the lobby beyond. Her cheeks were flushed, but now that the reading was over and had been well received—overwhelmingly so—she was relieved and more at ease.

No sooner had she stepped out of the ballroom than the sound of a footstep behind made her turn around, resigned to be accosted by yet another admirer.

"You are quite the sensation of the hour," Damian told her.

"Damian!" She smiled hesitantly in spite of his unwelcoming stance. "I had no notion you were here or even in London."

"How could you?" he asked without returning her smile. "How long is it since we last saw each other? Five years?"

"More like six, I fancy."

Several people passed by, eyeing the meeting with idle curiosity, but Stacia had eyes only for her brother, whose hairline was beginning to recede, and to her dismay she noted he had become quite plump in the years since she had left Brackentree.

"It's good to see you, Damian."

"I wish I could say the same of you, Eustacia."

Her smile faltered. "What a cruel thing to say after all these years apart."

"That was your wish, not mine, remember? And

103

success or not, you are an *actress*. Need I remind you it is not at all the thing for a lady of breeding?"

"Would you have had me starve instead? I was obliged to find a means to live, Damian, and a fortuitous encounter with a troupe of traveling actors showed me the way."

"Not that way, surely not that way."

"Let us not get into a brangle over that. Tell me how you are faring. You look to be in fine fettle. How is Peggy?"

"Well enough, but Uncle Quentin slipped the wind two years ago."

"I am truly sorry to hear you say so," Stacia responded.

"Peggy and I have three children. Three fine sons."

"I have three nephews," Stacia repeated in wonder, her smile returning. "How I should like to meet them."

The young man frowned. "I don't believe that would be a wise move, Eustacia, in the circumstances."

Her face grew stiff. "You have become exceedingly toplofty since we last met. Perhaps you always were and I never noted it. I wonder why you came here, feeling as you do about me."

"In truth I had not intended to make myself known to you—Peg would be horrified if she knew we were conversing—but I received an invitation, and it would not do to refuse Lady Charlotte Fitch-Drummond."

Stacia's face twisted into an expression of disgust. "You truly are a toadeater, Damian. Now I recall the way you always used to grease Uncle
104

Quentin's boots. I always wondered how you could do so."

"It might have gone better with you if you'd chosen to be more accommodating instead of always seeking to be disobliging."

Stacia drew herself up to full height. Fortunately Damian was not in the least tall and was unable to intimidate her with his height, unlike Lord Silverwood.

"If refusing to marry Mr. Chark was disobliging, I make no apology for it."

"In any event you have no cause to criticize me, Eustacia. You have become a castaway. Needless to say, no one here is aware you are my sister, and I would prefer it to remain our secret."

Stacia's face twisted into a knowing smile. "You have nothing to fear from me, Damian. If you do not boast of the connection, you may be assured I certainly will not. I am the toast of the town. My situation has been elevated beyond yours, I fancy."

As she turned on her heel, hiding the deep hurt her brother's attitude caused her, a group of people known to Damian passed by. He smiled and nodded to them, and it must have appeared that he and Stacia were enjoying an intimate discussion. She would have gone back into the ballroom, only as soon as they were alone again, her brother caught her by the arm and drew her back toward him.

"It isn't too late," he whispered. "You could give up this life." As she began to protest, Sir Hubert Patch went by, glancing at them curiously. When he'd gone by, Damian added, "You would then be very welcome in our house, Eustacia. You could even have a home with us and not need to stoop to all this nonsense any longer."

105

She was aghast. "Nonsense!" she echoed. "La! Have you seen all those people hanging on to my every word? Have you heard their praise or read the theatrical journals?"

Damian Farramond placed one finger under his neck cloth as if to loosen it slightly. "That is all well and good for any bit of muslin, but not you, Eustacia. You are a Farramond. Our mother was a Gilbert of Driffield."

"Much good it has done me," she told him, and her bitterness was very plain for him to see.

"Nevertheless, the offer stands. Give up this ... kind of life and you are guaranteed a home with us."

"If only you had made that offer before I ran away."

Continuing to look uncomfortable, he replied, "I offer it now, Eustacia, and I urge you to accept. You could make yourself useful to Peggy and the boys—"

Stacia let out a gasp of exasperation. "No doubt I could, but would any of you be useful to me? I think not."

So saying, she tore her arm away from his importuning hand and hurried away, only to come face-to-face with Lord Silverwood almost immediately. Before she had any chance to compose herself after Damian's setdown, she was immediately subjected to the earl's discomfiting scrutiny, centered, it seemed, on the low décolletage of her new gown. Even though she was fully dressed and clutched a Norwich silk shawl about her shoulders, she felt as unclothed as she had that day in her dressing room, clad in only a shift, and she wished she had placed a fichu in the neckline of her gown. As before, his eyes seemed all-seeing and caused her cheeks to blush, much to her annoyance.

In the few seconds' silence that spread between them like a chasm, Stacia wondered if she might step aside and pass him without speaking, but then Lady Charlotte glided up to them and slipped her arm into his in a proprietary manner that irked the younger woman.

"Miss Gilbert, you have yet to become acquainted with my brother, Lord Silverwood, I think."

"Your brother, ma'am?" Stacia repeated, feeling stupid.

The earl's lips quirked into a now familiar ironic smile. "Indeed yes. Lottie is my sister. It must be difficult for you to comprehend how a man like me could have so ravishing and charming a relative."

Stacia couldn't help but smile in response, for he had read her mind perfectly.

Unaware of any undercurrent between the two, Lady Charlotte laughed. "You must be warned, Miss Gilbert, Blaise has a rare way with Spanish coin. He will try to seduce you with his charm if he can."

"He can try," Stacia answered sweetly, "but I doubt if he could succeed, even with a veritable treasure chest of Spanish coin."

When she moved away, Lady Charlotte looked amazed. "Do you know, Blaise, my dear, I believe Miss Gilbert has thrown down the gauntlet to you, and I have it in mind she means exactly what she said!"

TEN

When supper was announced, Stacia was inundated by a large number of gentlemen who wished to escort her. She was glad enough to allow all of them to show her the way, feeling they acted like a guard of honor between her and Lord Silverwood, even though she was certain he would not approach her again. On the two occasions she had been unfortunate enough to encounter him in London, it had been purely accidental, and she determined to be vigilant in the future so it was not likely to occur again.

On the way to the supper room she passed the earl in conversation with Sir Hubert Patch. Neither gentleman looked up at her, but she was certainly aware of Lord Silverwood despite his apparent disregard of her and her large retinue of admirers.

"I saw you conversing with the Tragedy Queen," Sir Hubert was saying to his friend. "I was wondering what your intentions toward her were."

The earl managed to look considerably surprised. "I thought I had made myself perfectly clear on that score, Hu. I have no intentions whatsoever."

"I thought that now she is the most celebrated actress currently in town ..."

"That is of no account to me," his lordship replied, his countenance growing darker at the recollection. "One rebuff is quite sufficient."

Sir Hubert looked skeptical. "You always play your cards close to your chest, Sil, so I don't mind declaring an interest and saying I'd have a wager on it if you do intend to pay court to her."

"Rely upon it, Hu, I don't intend to act the moon-calf over that little brimstone."

Sir Hubert laughed. "Never thought you would go *that* far, Sil, but I considered pride might come into it. It's not like you to cry off at the first fence or to pocket an affront so easily."

"Believe me, Hu, you're entirely beside the bridle on this one. Miss Gilbert is of no interest to me, I assure you."

"Just as well," Sir Hubert responded, nodding his head in a satisfied manner.

"Why are you so interested in my intentions?" the earl asked, looking suddenly amused. "Do you intend to try and curry favor on your own behalf?"

The other man looked a little abashed. "She's beyond my touch, I fancy, although I have it in mind her interests are well and truly fixed, and although I suspected it wouldn't take long, I confess I am somewhat surprised at who she has taken color with, given the choice of top-sawyers who have set up pursuit."

The earl folded his arms as he leaned back against the wall and regarded his friend from beneath his long, dark eyelashes. "Oh? What gives you the notion she's sweet on someone?"

"I saw her, after the recitation, in a very intimate coze with none other than Mr. Farramond."

"Damian Farramond!" Lord Silverwood exclaimed. Then he laughed. "That fubsy-faced mushroom. The woman must have more sense than to make sheep's eyes in his direction."

"I thought you had taken him up and were intent upon polishing off his rustic edges."

The earl's lip curled derisively. "What gave you that outlandish notion?"

"I've seen him hanging on to your coattails frequently of late, that is all."

"He has tried, but that is only because he's a toady. He can't possibly be sweet on the Tragedy Queen, Hu. I always considered him petticoat-led by that horse-faced wife of his."

"So did I, but she's a fetching little baggage, as you'll be the first to agree." His lordship's countenance grew dark again. "I know what I saw."

Lord Silverwood was thoughtful for a moment or two, and then he slapped his friend on the back, saying, "Come, Hu, let us partake of some supper. Lottie always does her guests proud."

"I recall you are correct on that score, and we mustn't for anything allow tattle to get in the way of a good supper, especially as I'm beginning to feel sharp-set. Even the ladies don't go that far."

In the supper room Stacia was beginning to relax once more. Even though she was aware that most of those about her were purely sycophantic, it was pleasant to bask in approval after the years of disdain from Uncle Quentin and those who were fearful of her ability in the Gala Troupe.

As soon as Lord Silverwood entered the room, she became aware of him. He was tall enough to be seen in any crowd, and although she was reluctant to admit the fact, even to herself, he did, invariably, appear elegant in the restrained style made popular by Beau Brummell. How she wished there were

110

nothing to admire in him, but she could find no fault with his appearance, even if his character left much to be desired.

Although others constantly claimed her attention and she did contrive to attend them, she was also, much to her own annoyance, aware of every move Lord Silverwood made. When he came closer, pausing to exchange a few words with various guests, who did not appear to share Stacia's disgust of him, she became uncomfortable again, hoping he would stay some distance away from her. Even without actually conversing with him, she found his closeness abhorrent.

When he was standing almost close enough to touch her, he was accosted by a vapid blonde, who, by evidence of her simpering manner, had set her cap at him.

"How I wish I could recite so well as Miss Gilbert," the girl sighed.

"I have no possible doubt you can, Miss Seymour," he responded, adopting a careless manner.

The buffet contained all manner of delicacies, but suddenly Stacia's appetite deserted her, and she handed her plate to one of the footmen moving round the room.

The girl simpered and blushed to the roots of her hair. "Lord Silverwood, you mustn't say so."

"Why not? Reciting poetry is in no way remarkable. It is something at which I believe all ladies to be proficient."

The young lady chuckled. "You must be roasting me, my lord."

"Your wit encourages it in me, ma'am."

Unaware of the irony of his words, she went on to ask, "How is dear Lady Silverwood?"

"In excellent health and spirits, I thank you," the earl replied, and when Stacia sneaked a brief glance at him, she noted that his features were stiff with boredom.

"I did look to see her here. I do so enjoy a coze with her ladyship."

"She has decided to remain in the country for the time being, but I will certainly convey your regard when next I see her."

Stacia smiled to herself, sympathizing heartily with the absent Lady Silverwood for wanting to put as many miles as possible between her and her rake of a husband.

The blonde he referred to as Miss Seymour kept up an adoring conversation, complimenting the earl on every possible matter. Stacia's head was just about level with his shoulder, and after a while, when she found his proximity to her totally unbearable, she quickly excused herself from her admirers and began to make her way out of the supper room.

She'd been hoping to slip away unseen, but Lady Charlotte intercepted her before she could locate Maura, who was enjoying as much attention as her friend.

"My dear Miss Gilbert," Lady Charlotte greeted her, "having you here has been a complete delight."

"To me, too, my lady," Stacia responded, trying to hide her anxiety to be gone.

"Everyone I have spoken to is unanimous in singing your praises."

Unanimous? Stacia asked herself. There was at least the one who dissented, she was sure, and she would be glad of it. The last thing she wanted was Lord Silverwood as an admirer.

"I wonder if I might prevail upon you a little

longer?" Lady Charlotte was asking, and Stacia gave the woman her attention once again. "Would you be kind enough to sing for us before you go?"

"Really, I . . ."

"It would be so much appreciated by everyone. I fear that once you are gone, you will be too heavily committed to return in the near future."

Stacia didn't argue on that point. In the future she would require a good deal of persuasion to enter any building where Lord Silverwood was likely to be.

"We must be prepared to depart as soon as I have finished my song," Stacia whispered to Maura as the room began to fill again in expectation of an extra treat.

"I'll go now to fetch your cloak and wait for you in the hall downstairs," Maura promised. "I'm not in the least surprised you're fatigued; you have had a full day with your performance and a morning of rehearsals before it. I shall make certain the carriage is waiting outside; but it has been a wonderful evening, has it not? You have been a triumph!"

Stacia contrived to smile halfheartedly before she hurried to the orchestra dais at one end of the massive ballroom. The room became immediately hushed when a young lady seated herself at the pianoforte. A moment later Stacia began to sing, rushing slightly, but no one seemed to notice her haste.

"Early one morning just as the sun was rising,
I saw a maiden
singing in the valley below."

Her voice rang out sweet and clear until her gaze leveled upon Lord Silverwood standing at the back of the room, his attention—like everyone else's—concentrated on her, only the scrutiny of the entire roomful of people did not trouble her as his did. He was like a thorn that had slipped beneath her skin and constantly pained her.

Her voice faltered momentarily before her professionalism took over, and she continued to sing well, certain no one had noticed the brief lapse.

"Oh, don't deceive me, oh, never leave me.
How could you use a poor maiden so?"

The applause she received was enthusiastic, and it took her some minutes to progress through the room. When she did at last reach the entrance after bidding farewell to Lady Charlotte, it was with a feeling of great relief.

The evening had been a considerable triumph for her and would be proclaimed as such in the salons of the ton, and yet Lord Silverwood had contrived to cast a shadow over it, just as he had over more than half her life.

Her relief at the ending of the evening was short-lived when she heard her name spoken softly by the very gentleman who she felt blighted her existence, and she turned round on her heel to face the object of her torment yet again.

"Leaving so soon, Miss Gilbert, in the hour of your triumph?"

"It has been a hectic day, and I'm due onstage early tomorrow for rehearsals," she replied without meeting his gaze.

Whenever she looked at him, she was afraid she would not be able to hide her emotions, which—unusual for her—were difficult to control whenever she was obliged to be in his presence. Such occasions were too many of late for her comfort.

It was always a great temptation for her to tell him exactly how she felt about him and why, but Stacia was happier hugging her hatred to herself. Explained, it might lose some of its passion; she didn't want anything to have that effect. Her hatred of him had sustained her for so long. As Maura had pointed out, she was comfortable with it.

"When I saw you acting in Dorrington at so tender an age, I would never have imagined that one day you'd have London at your feet. You have my profound admiration for your achievement."

She began to move away from him, murmuring, "Lord Silverwood, I don't want your admiration."

"You bask in the admiration of others readily enough."

"I advise you to save your moonshine for those who would appreciate it."

His face took on the wooden look she had seen on that occasion in her dressing room, and it occurred to her now that he would make an unforgiving enemy, but Stacia was beyond caring. He could harm her no more than he had harmed her all those years ago. He could take nothing more from her than he had taken then.

"All this flummery has truly turned your head, hasn't it?" he asked in a low, even voice that sounded menacing to Stacia's receptive ears, and she turned on her heel to face the object of her torment yet again.

Before she could do or say anything further, he had reached out, drawing her toward him. Her eyes were wide and questioning, his searching her face

115

with disturbing ferocity. He did not know about the fountain of bitterness from which her hatred gushed endlessly.

When she was almost close enough for their faces to touch and Stacia felt her head swim, he whispered, "I have a mind to tumble you from the heights of your arrogance, my fair beauty. I could so easily humble you."

Before the fearful Stacia could wrench herself from his clutches, he had pulled her against him in a viselike grip. She could feel his strength against her, making her seem weak by comparison. His lips claimed hers in a cruel and seeking kiss. Her heart had begun beating fast from the moment his hand had touched her flesh, but the effect of his lips upon hers was like that of a flint spark on tinder, turning her blood to molten metal, gushing through her veins and igniting her entire soul in a conflagration that threatened to consume her entirely.

Although the kiss lasted only a few moments, it could have been a lifetime. Every moment of it was to become burned into her memory. Whenever the recollection was conjured up in her mind, her senses felt the hardness of his body as he held her against him.

Later she was to wonder if she could have struggled free of his grip, but she knew it would have been useless.

At last, when he thrust her away from him, he smiled in triumph, and her face became suffused with fury. She was angry at his presumption, but even more with herself for succumbing, be it only for those few seconds. What was worse, he *knew* she had submitted to him, and she was speechless with shame.

Her cheeks, she was aware, had become flushed with color, and tears of frustration welled into her eyes at her own humiliation at his hand. With all the force she could muster, she brought her hand up and struck it across his face before turning on her heel and rushing down the stairs, where she desperately hoped Maura would be waiting so they could leave without a second's further delay.

ELEVEN

The memory of that kiss and its unexpected effect upon her would not allow Stacia any peace at all. Her only relief was slipping into another character every evening at the theater, which she did with renewed vigor, and that, ironically, revived the commendation of her acting.

Her popularity among the ton and the theater-going public kept growing as word of her performances spread. She was besieged by admirers wherever she went, which mollified her to a great degree, but her desire to do Lord Silverwood down in some measure grew apace.

Callers at the house were received graciously, and Stacia was glad of their presence to divert her mind from thoughts of the earl—which, since the night of the soiree, seemed to fill it more than ever.

After several days passed without seeing or hearing mention of his name, she began to relax again, lecturing herself sternly on the folly of allowing that man to color her life for the second time. She decided she would act in a sensible manner and not permit him to spoil her newfound success and prosperity.

A letter from Brighton cheered her somewhat when it arrived. "Ormerod and Marietta have settled well into their new home and don't miss all the traveling they were used to," Maura pointed out when she came to read it.

"I shouldn't be at all surprised if, before long, the Prince Regent is wiping his eyes of his tears after one of their performances," Stacia rejoined. "They may not miss the traveling, but I fancy they cannot possibly give up the life for very long."

Stacia quickly penned a reply to them, recounting her own exciting life in London, save for the incident with Lord Silverwood, which she fully intended to forget, while Maura stepped out to purchase a frank so the missive could be dispatched without delay.

The letter had only just been finished when the arrival of Paris Kingswell was announced. Stacia greeted him warmly. He was one gentleman with whom she always felt totally at ease.

"Paris, how nice of you to call."

He smiled bashfully. "I wondered if you might be heartily tired of my company after enduring it each time you're at the theater."

"Not at all, I assure you!"

"I was passing by—almost past the door—and thought I would stop to inquire of your health."

Stacia looked surprised. "I'm in plump currant, I thank you."

"So I see. It's a great relief to hear that slight hoarseness has gone from your voice. It was a concern to me, you can be sure."

The reminder was not a welcome one, for she recalled after her return from Lady Charlotte's soiree she had wept so copiously into her pillow, her voice had been hoarse during the following performance, a failing on the part of her professional integrity, and she vowed never to allow it to happen again.

119

Dismissing the memory once and for all, she smiled at Paris, and he became flustered. " 'Twas nothing, my dear, I assure you. Maura plied me with drinks of lemon and honey, and now I'm as right as a trivet. Won't you stay a while and take nuncheon with me?"

He was already moving toward the door. "No, I thank you. I must be on my way, but I shall see you this evening—*Candide*."

She smiled again as he used the name of her new character in a lighter type of play this time, one that she was thoroughly enjoying playing.

"Until then, *Maxime*," she responded in like tones before they both dissolved in laughter.

When he reached the door, he paused to say, "Ah, yes. I almost forgot to make mention of it, Stacia. Your fame has reached new heights in this town." As she looked at him expectantly, he went on, "Burlington—*Lord* Burlington, that is—signed me in to White's after the performance last night. Recall you didn't wish to go to supper with me." He put one hand up as she began to protest her fatigue. "I do understand, my dear. In any event it was a most pleasant evening, even if I did prefer to be with you. The supper was exceedingly enjoyable, too. They engage an excellent chef at White's, although when some of the gamesters find time to eat I cannot conceive. Mayhap Lord Sandwich had the right notion in taking his supper between two slices of bread so he need not leave the table. Afterward we indulged in a game of piquet—"

"Paris, you're going on like a bagpipe. What has this to do with me?"

"Ah, yes, indeed." He cast her an apologetic smile. "As I was leaving and the steward was fetching my cloak and hat, I happened to glance in the betting book. It was there on the steward's table, open for all to see, I might tell you." He frowned. "Trent wagered on Turnberry to win the derby. I wonder if I might have a few guineas on the nag. . . ."

"Paris!" Stacia urged, beginning to feel exasperated.

The actor looked at her again. "It was then that I saw it."

"What, Paris? What on earth did you see?"

He closed his eyes, the better to concentrate on the recollection. "Willard wagers Traynor a monkey that Silverwood will win the heart of the Tragedy Queen within thirty days of this one."

Stacia looked aghast, her ready smile fading as he spoke. She was aware, from her father's gambling days, that a monkey amounted to five hundred pounds.

"How dare they?" she cried.

"Don't take it too personally, my dear. It's quite an honor, don't you know?"

"An honor? This unsavory revelation has done nothing save put me in a fine pelter. Am I truly supposed to be *pleased*?"

The actor was unperturbed by her outrage. "You'll soon grow used to the ways of these men of the town, my dear. If an actress takes with the most prominent of the fashionables, she is made, and let me tell you, my dear, it has already happened to you. You must grow used to this kind of attention, but if it puts you in such a pet, I wish I hadn't made mention of it."

"I'm indebted to you, Paris, for the information,"

121

she told him soberly, and he ventured a hesitant smile. "That's the barber. I shall see you anon."

When he had gone, Stacia let out a most unlady-like howl of fury. Paris Kingswell might consider the wager an honor, but Stacia's anger and frustration knew no bounds. After pacing clumsily around the room for some minutes, she hurried upstairs to fetch her new velvet pelisse with the gold epaulets and matching frogged fastenings, together with the shako-styled bonnet that matched it and was said to become her. Tying the strings of her bonnet with trembling fingers, she dashed out of the house and hailed a passing hackney carriage.

Lord Silverwood's mansion, she knew, was situated on Park Lane, so she gave the jarvey the directions and then sat back, oblivious to the malodorous air in the carriage, tapping her fingers impatiently on her reticule and fuming silently at yet another incidence of the earl's ill-usage of her. This time, however, the matter could not be more public, and it was not to be borne. Gentlemen of Lord Silverwood's standing considered themselves above civilized behavior, but she vowed he would be obliged to learn on this occasion he was not. How she was to tackle him once she arrived she had no notion. Anger propelled her, and Stacia had no thoughts beyond that.

The journey took some considerable time, owing to the number of carriages on Oxford Street, and that added substantially to her anger and impatience. How long before the abominable wager was scandal broth in all the drawing rooms of the ton? she asked herself. Her every move would be scrutinized with even more attention than now. Being in the same building as Lord Silverwood, even if she did not clap eyes upon him, would be a greater agony than ever before.

"It is not to be borne," she murmured as the hackney carriage drew up beneath the porte cochère of the earl's mansion.

A footman sprang forward to help her down, although Stacia was already getting out unaided, so great was her need to confront the earl. The lackey looked at her askance, and she supposed that ladies who visited his master did not usually arrive by hackney carriage.

"Is his lordship home?" she asked after ensuring that the jarvey would wait for her.

"Yes, ma'am, but I'm afraid—"

"Kindly inform him Miss Gilbert wishes to speak with him on a matter of great import. *If you please*," she added when the fellow hesitated.

Her authoritative tone had the desired effect, and he hurried away up the curving staircase, leaving Stacia to kick her heels in the great marble hallway.

Despite her agitation she was able to appreciate the full splendor of the house, with its marble statuary, Venetian paintings, and soaring rotunda in which she stood. Lord Silverwood was in need of Dover's End in much the same way as a lame and mangy horse was required to pull his carriage. All around her were signs of wealth and plenty, and yet he had not hesitated to take what little was left of the Farramond fortune.

To her relief she was obliged to hold her anger for only a short while before the earl came down the stairs. He was dressed, she noted, to his usual standard of elegance, in a buff-colored coat that fitted his manly shoulders perfectly and stockinette

123

pantaloons that clung perfectly without a wrinkle to his calves. The memory of being held against him manifested itself once again when she saw him, but Stacia made a valiant effort to dismiss it from her mind, a necessity if she was to comport herself with any composure whatsoever. However, she was unable to prevent her cheeks from becoming slightly flushed, and she was obliged to avert her eyes from his.

She waited for him to come down the stairs, her anger making her bold. He passed paintings of long-dead ancestors, many of whose haughty features bore a striking resemblance to the present-day incumbent of the Silverwood title.

When he was halfway down the stairs, he asked unsmilingly, "To what do I owe this unexpected pleasure, Miss Gilbert?"

"Outrage, my lord."

"Then I fancy nothing has changed, but you do not mince words, I'll grant you that."

"My feelings of injustice make it a trifle difficult to grease your boots in the manner to which you are evidently accustomed, but I'm persuaded that before long you will find a score of females who are more than willing to do so."

"Let's cut line, Miss Gilbert. I own you are entitled to be off the hooks with me, but I'm bound to tell you my cheek continues to bear the imprint of your hand. Would you care to come closer and see for yourself?"

Immediately she flinched. "I am not usually given to such behavior, my lord. You must own you were deserving of the castigation."

"Oh, I do," he answered, still unsmiling.

"To harp on it any further would only imbue the

unfortunate episode with an import it does not bear. I am more concerned at present with weightier matters."

He reached the last step and smiled without mirth as he came toward her. It was all she could do to stand her ground. The temptation to back away from him, despite her bold statement, was almost too great to resist.

"Let us cross swords no more. I had intended to send a note to your lodgings inviting you to ride out with me this afternoon, so I may in some small way try to make amends for my abominable behavior the other evening. I trust you will not take offense at that small gesture of contrition."

He had a way with words, she granted, so much so that she almost believed him to be contrite, but then she reminded herself of the purpose of her visit.

"I regret I am already engaged for this afternoon."

He emitted an almost imperceptible sigh. "I expected no less. So what does bring you to my door, Miss Gilbert? Another scolding perhaps? Yes, I fear you are about to ring a peal over me. I see it plainly written on your countenance."

She was furious that as an actress she should know how to conceal emotion as well as express it, yet he found her as transparent as her shift that night in Dorrington.

He put his head slightly to one side as if to consider her. "You really are quite lovely, Miss Gilbert. If only you didn't always scowl at me, you could even be considered a beauty."

"Oh, you are outside of enough!" she gasped, and she did back away from him.

"Perhaps, but am I as truly obnoxious as you appear to believe?" he asked in such a mild manner that she was forced to look at him again. "In most circles I am held to be pleasant, even obliging. I cannot conceive why you have taken me in dislike."

"Can you not?" she responded through clenched teeth.

"No, I truly cannot. I have gone out of my way to be amiable toward you to no avail. You will never discover my better nature if you won't allow me to show it to you."

"Lord Silverwood, I don't wish to take up more of your valuable time than is absolutely necessary. . . ."

"That is most considerate of you, ma'am" was his emollient reply.

Stacia bit back her irritation and determined not to allow him to rouse her to anger, something he could do with so much ease. "It has come to my notice that there is a wager in the betting book at White's, and although my name is not actually mentioned, it is perfectly clear who is the object of the bet."

His gentle, ironic smile faded. "I regret you have come to hear of it."

Aghast, she retorted, "So you *do* know of it?"

"One of your most ardent admirers, Mr. Damian Farramond, brought the matter to my attention in no uncertain terms less than an hour ago."

She started at the mention of her brother's name. "Damian Farramond," she echoed.

"You are, I'm aware, acquainted with the gentleman, who has taken it upon himself to act Sir Galahad. I trust you do not take his behavior amiss. I recall you were seen in a lengthy coze with that

126

gentleman the evening of my sister's soiree," he reminded her, "so there can be no secret about his partiality."

"You put entirely the wrong construction on the incident," Stacia was quick to assure him, ignoring the now familiar irony in his tone. "He is a bore, however, and insisted upon discussing with me every dramatic role he had ever seen, before I was able to make good my escape. . . ."

Her voice faded away beneath his questioning look when she realized she was prattling on about Damian beyond what was necessary. It came as some relief for her to acknowledge the earl really did believe Damian only an admirer. He probably believed him to be her *chèr ami*, but that was preferable to the truth, although she doubted that her sister-in-law would think so. Being known as either his sister or his *chère amie* would overset Peggy Farramond.

"You may rest assured, Miss Gilbert, that I was just about to depart and confront the two gentlemen responsible and make them withdraw the wager from the book."

"I am most obliged to you, my lord," she murmured, averting her eyes again.

"Obliged, eh?" he mocked. "Well, we make progress, I think."

Choking back her irritation once more, she at last allowed herself to move away from his overpowering presence. "Now that the matter is about to be resolved to the satisfaction of all parties involved, I intend to detain you no longer. Good day, my lord."

He followed closely on her heels as she hurried toward the door, and when he saw the hackney carriage outside, he said, "You must allow me to take you home, Miss Gilbert. Traveling in a hackney carriage is not for our leading theatrical lady."

Once again her cheeks grew pink. "Being seen in yours, my lord, would only give sustenance to Lord Willard."

Stacia didn't know what caused her to pause when she reached the door. Perhaps because of his effort to be obliging for once, it was a desire not to make her dislike of him too obvious—but when she did hesitate, he took her hand and raised it to his lips, meeting her startled look with an amused one of his own.

"Traynor is a complete fool even to contemplate taking up Willard's wager," he told her as he carefully caressed her hand before he allowed it to drop. "If I were in the least interested in winning your heart, he should have sufficient knowledge of me to know the result would be a foregone conclusion."

TWELVE

By the time Stacia arrived back at the house in Tavistock Square, she was no more mollified than when she had left, and because she had departed from Silverwood House in such a lather of indignation, she had instructed the jarvey to drive around until she was calm enough to return home.

"I was concerned for you when I returned and found you gone," Maura confided, casting Stacia a curious look. "Mary said Mr. Kingswell had called and you'd gone straight out afterward—in a hackney carriage."

As she stripped off her gloves, hat, and pelisse, Stacia heatedly recounted her reason for dashing off in so precipitate a manner.

"And," she added in outraged tones as she flung her reticule down on a chair, "he had the effrontery to believe I might go riding with him in the park this afternoon! That was truly outside of enough!"

"If Lord Silverwood has offered to make right the matter, I cannot conceive why you are in such a pelter now. I don't understand why you wouldn't wish to go with him this afternoon."

Calmer now, Stacia replied, "No, I daresay you don't."

"From all I heard when I was at Lady Charlotte's

129

house the other evening, Lord Silverwood is the most sought-after man in town."

"I do wonder what Lady Silverwood feels about that."

Maura looked taken aback. "I hadn't considered he might be married."

"You may be certain I have it on very good authority that the poor creature exists. He lives a bachelor life here in town while poor Lady Silverwood remains hidden away in the country. I'll wager she's a mousy little heiress with a king's ransom in property for her portion. In truth, Maura, I'd liefer go riding with one of the apes in the Tower Menagerie than the Earl of Silverwood!"

"Well, I believe that is coming it too strong." Maura looked at her friend for some few moments as Stacia stared into the fireplace, her thoughts far away. Then she said, "Stacia, my dear, I really never have understood your hatred—for that is what it is—of Lord Silverwood, who appears to me a charming and most attractive man. I am persuaded you have your reasons, which I wouldn't presume to press you to reveal, but if you do wish to best him in whatever duel of strength you are engaging in"—Stacia looked at her curiously—"it seems to me it might be better if you became a little more amenable toward him. It isn't possible to best anyone from a distance. You could do worse than accept his offer to take you riding in his phaeton. . . ."

"It is out of the question," Stacia snapped, looking away again. "I can't abide the man, and I won't spend another second in his company. It's disagreeable enough to know we reside in the same town as each other, let alone share a seat in a phaeton."

130

The older woman sighed profoundly. "It was just a consideration. You are so sought-after of late, so many gentlemen vie for your favor."

"For what reason?" Stacia asked, unable to hide her bitterness. "It is only because I am fashionable and they live in hope I might become their *chère amie*. Actresses are considered fair game, objects of wagers, to be used as and when a gentleman wishes. I shall have none of it, I tell you!"

"Whatever the reason, you possess a very potent weapon in your armory."

Once again Stacia looked at her curiously, and Maura shrugged. "All his peers must be aware he is in the forefront of those who are seeking your favor."

"I do wonder how many private wagers there are. It is not to be borne!"

"It is if you are able to turn the matter to your own advantage, my dear. You could easily gain his public humiliation by making it appear initially that you look sweet upon him and then very obviously rejecting him. Giving him turnips would be a grievous blow to such a proud man."

When Maura had gone to check on their nuncheon, Stacia sank down onto the window seat, staring out into the square, cast deep into thought.

"If I were in the least interested . . ."

His words echoed in her mind, mocking her. He was a man who liked to meddle with people's emotions. Well, so she would interfere with his and enjoy the outcome.

After a while, she went to her desk and began to write a hurried note to be dispatched immediately. The moment the note had been dispatched, Stacia regretted her impetuosity. Acting the spoon to the

131

Earl of Silverwood, even for a limited period, was going to stretch her ingenuity as an actress to the very limit. Only the thought of him being publicly humiliated drove her on. He might well have a mind to humble her, but he would soon enough discover the bitter taste of that situation for himself, she vowed.

However, by the time his high-perch phaeton drew up outside the house, determination had reasserted itself, and she watched until he had entered the house. She could hear him conversing with Maura in the drawing room, no doubt charming her with his moonshine. Stacia knew she could not be swayed, which imbued her with a new sense of power, and after allowing him to languish for an unconscionable time, she came down to join them.

She was wearing her newest pelisse in rose pink velvet with a matching poke-brim bonnet decorated with curled ostrich feathers and lined with pleated silk. When she entered the drawing room, he got to his feet, and his admiring look, Stacia was satisfied to acknowledge, was real enough.

"Miss Gilbert," he greeted her, again taking her hand and raising it to his lips, "you look truly ravishing."

She considered he, too, looked handsome, clad in a caped greatcoat and Hessian boots. Casting such thoughts out of her mind, she dimpled prettily, slipping easily into the role she had cast for herself.

"I thank you, sir." She smiled conspiratorially at Maura. "Let us not waste any more of this spring sunshine, my lord. I fear I have kept you kicking your heels for far too long."

"It is worth the wait, so you must think nothing of it. It is a lady's prerogative to be tardy, and in any event Mrs. Copeland has kept me admirably entertained in your absence."

"The pleasure was mine," Maura responded, and Stacia wasn't in the least gratified to know she meant it.

When he was about to hand Stacia up to the box, he suddenly frowned. "Much as it pleases me to have your company, Miss Gilbert, I confess I was somewhat surprised to receive your note. After our previous encounters it was not what I expected."

Stacia feigned bashfulness. "It has all been the most appalling mistake on my behalf, at least where my refusal this morning was concerned. In my understandable agitation this morning I was absolutely certain it was today I was engaged to go to Bullock's Museum with Mr. French. When I returned home, I discovered to my utter dismay it is tomorrow that I am engaged to accompany him, so you can observe, my lord, I can be such a chucklehead at times."

The earl looked disbelieving, but nevertheless he replied, "I cannot possibly concur with that particular appraisal of your nature but confess it is my good fortune that you are, after all, free. I'm relieved to find you don't harbor any grudges toward me for my occasional lapses of gentlemanly behavior."

"Indeed not," she assured him as warmly as she could contrive. " 'Tis impossible, in any event, to do so in all conscience. It would be churlish of me not to accept so genuine an apology, and you have no doubt made right the matter of the indelicate wager we discussed this morning."

"You may be sure that I have," he told her as he climbed up on the box beside her. "The gentlemen involved will tender their apologies to you themselves in no uncertain terms. I insisted upon it."

"Oh, how kind of you to trouble. The matter is satisfactorily resolved, and I'm so glad I found it possible to accept an invitation from the elevated Lord Silverwood."

"I know you not to be a toady, Miss Gilbert," he remarked, glancing at her as he set the carriage in motion with only the slightest flick of his whip, "so I am confident it is for my sake you have come with me, and not for any gain to your standing."

Stacia bridled slightly at the implication but quickly pacified herself, for she knew she must cast out, if only temporarily, her hatred of this man. Time enough to enjoy the luxury of glorying in it when she contrived to bring him down from the heights of his overweening pride.

"I feel," she said in a measured tone, "I have wronged you in great measure." She stole a glance at him from beneath her lowered lashes in a way considered flirtatious. "I beg you to understand why we started out with daggers drawn. It was all most unfortunate."

"I have attempted to understand it myself," he answered, "and have been able to find no answer that satisfies me."

Stacia folded her gloved hands in her lap and told him, "I believe myself at fault entirely, although, as I intend to explain, there are mitigating circumstances. For so many years the Gala Troupe performed to no real acclaim. . . ."

"Until you joined their ranks."

"How kind of you to say so," she simpered before going on. "Up until the evening you called upon me in my dressing room, I was totally unused to any-

134

one's attentions, let alone those of a fashionable gentleman like yourself."

"I was simply moved by the pathos of your performance."

"Oh, dear." She sighed. "How dreadful of me to assume you had designs on my virtue."

"Heaven forfend" was his straight-faced response.

"Lord Silverwood, the plain truth is that I was frightened of the attention I was at last receiving. After so many years of anonymity onstage, my fear made me churlish. That is my justification, and I beg you to accept it as the truth of the matter."

"So simple," he responded, shaking his head sadly. "It was crass of me not to note it at the time, although your acting was so fine, I had no way of knowing you were a mere novice. How sad it put a barrier between us for so long, but what a relief to know it is all behind us and only companionship lies ahead."

He turned to bestow upon her a smile, and she felt herself stiffen with alarm. Her heart had quite unexpectedly begun to beat faster. Caution, she told herself. It was all a pretense, and she knew she must not allow his charm to penetrate her guard. It was, after all, only make-believe, just as it was onstage.

"I do fully understand that it has been my own foolish behavior," she went on quickly, "that prompted your own less-than-chivalrous attitude toward me, but you have, I own, apologized profusely, and I readily accept my own culpability."

She gazed up at him and he smiled back at her, the very picture of mutual amicability.

"Tell me, Miss Gilbert, how did you come to take

to the boards? You must be aware that since you have become all the crack, the tattle-baskets want to know all about you, and precious little information is circulating about your origins. Mysterious ancestries exist only for the discovery as far as the gossips are concerned."

Initially the fear of questions being asked about her background fed her reluctance to join the Regency, but now she was more confident of keeping her origins a secret. She hoped so, for she feared her sister-in-law might die of shame if it became known she was so closely related to one of the acting classes, and Stacia didn't want for anything to have *that* on her conscience.

"There is no mystery about me, my lord. I was born into the life," she told him with a boldness that had no shame. "My mother was an actress, a very fine one, I am told. My father, alas, perished when I was but a babe, and in order to feed us both Mama was obliged to tour the country with me in her arms. I am told when I was very small, I slept contentedly in a drawer in her dressing room while she performed onstage. And then, when I was still a very small child, Mama contracted a putrid fever and slipped the wind, too, but before she died, she begged Mr. Ormerod Greaves to take care of me, which he did most handsomely. From a very tender age I had begun to make myself useful backstage and eventually took on small roles myself, encouraged in great measure by my dear friend, Mr. Greaves."

"What an inspiring tale, Miss Gilbert," the earl declared as they entered Hyde Park. "It is worthy of a stage melodrama in its own right."

Stacia cast him a suspicious look, but there was

nothing in his manner to indicate anything other than total belief in what she had told him.

Rotten Row was choked with carriages and more splendid horses than Stacia had ever seen in her entire life, and she was just admiring them when he added, "More remarkable is the fact you appear to have garnered an excellent education at the same time."

His remark was sufficient to jolt her out of her complacency with a start, but then she quickly explained, "My mother was an educated woman, and she taught me the rudiments between times."

"What a remarkable woman *she* must have been."

A great many people acknowledged the passage of the phaeton as it progressed slowly. Stacia nodded to all who greeted her, although there were few enough people she actually recognized. She was fascinated by the sight of so many ostentatious carriages that passed them by. Lord Silverwood's was quite restrained by comparison. *Elegant* was the word that tripped unwillingly into her mind. Everything about him could be considered elegant—at least when he was in an obliging mood. Stacia was bound to consider herself unfortunate in having witnessed him at his most diabolic, and she couldn't help but wonder what her feelings for him might have been if they had met for the first time when she came up to town.

One illustrious dowager greeted them, and Stacia snapped herself out of her reverie, for to allow her thoughts to go down such a path was to invite disaster.

Most of the ladies they encountered were clad in the latest fashions, some of which were quite out-

137

landish, while quite a few dowagers in landaus or barouches were dowdy and old-fashioned, but their elevated positions meant it didn't matter a jot.

The sight of Stacia in Lord Silverwood's phaeton caused no small amount of attention, just as it was intended to do. For once she wanted the prattle-boxes to spread the on-dit about her and Lord Silverwood. It would suit her purpose admirably if they were perceived as a pair. She wanted them to become the most talked-about couple in London.

Many of the glances she received from ladies were unmistakably envious ones, and it seemed supremely ironic to her that she was perhaps the only female in fashionable circles who wished she were not in the earl's phaeton. One advantage of the situation she did consider, however, was that if she was seen to be his *chère amie*, other young bucks vying for her affection might now desist.

As the earl's team picked its way through the throng of carriages, Stacia stiffened when she caught sight of one in particular, an open landau that was occupied by her sister-in-law, accompanied by one of her stiff-rumped acquaintances, and to her dismay she noted that it was coming toward them.

Mrs. Farramond's face froze into an expression of alarm, and although Stacia was amused to see her consternation, she did understand it. Peggy Farramond evidently envisaged all her social pretensions coming to nothing if the truth was revealed.

When the carriages at last came abreast, Mrs. Farramond nodded curtly to the earl, whom she would not wish to offend while ignoring his passenger entirely. What a terrible dilemma, Stacia thought as she carefully controlled her own feelings of amusement at the situation. Peggy's maid would no doubt be required to burn feathers for her mistress when she returned home in a state of near collapse.

"Oh, dear," Lord Silverwood lamented, with his customary irony evident in his manner, "I wonder what you have done to earn Mrs. Farramond's displeasure? That was as direct a cut as I have ever witnessed." He frowned then, and Stacia had a brief glimpse of the darker side of his nature. "I intend to make my own displeasure known to her at the first opportunity. It is beyond the bounds that any acquaintance of mine is treated in so cavalier a manner."

The thought of Peggy receiving one of his setdowns did not entirely displease her, but she replied, "Do not permit her to trouble your head, my lord. I assure you I am not cast into the dismals at being cut by that lady. She is, after all, of very little consequence to either of us."

"You are generous to a fault," he told her, casting her a curious look.

"You flatter me unnecessarily, my lord."

He bestowed upon her a devastating smile that momentarily made her look away in confusion. Recovering herself quickly, she silently vowed, *You will experience my "generosity" firsthand before long.*

"Mrs. Farramond is evidently a disagreeable female who disapproves of actresses," Stacia said aloud a moment later. "There are those who do, you know."

"I cannot imagine who would disapprove of you, Miss Gilbert. However, I daresay Mrs. Farramond is as disagreeable as her husband is agreeable to you."

Stacia couldn't reply without compromising her position, so she set her face forward, drew in a deep breath, and said, "How wonderful it is to be in London in the spring. Mrs. Copeland and I are so enjoying our stay. At every opportunity we have been around to museums, galleries, and all the usual sights. I daresay you would look upon it as deadly dull."

"It would depend a great deal on my companion on such expeditions."

Stacia dimpled shyly. "I cannot conceive why Lady Silverwood would wish to ruralize rather than be here with you in London at this glorious time of the year."

Momentarily the earl looked a little taken aback and then began to drive them back toward the gate, which came as a relief, for she was beginning to tire of her role. Acting a part in real life was much more of a strain than onstage, she was finding.

"My mother often feels her age nowadays," he explained a moment later. "She enjoys the pleasures of a rural existence much more than the delights of town."

"I did not mean your mother, my lord. I was referring to your wife."

"My wife!" Stacia smiled at causing him consternation. "It is flattering to think there might be a female willing to tolerate me as a spouse, but a wife is the one appendage I have never succeeded in acquiring."

It was Stacia's turn to be surprised. His mother. No wonder the little blond miss was pouring the
140

butterboat over him. She must have been greasing his boots about his *mother*.

"I am evidently in error," she stammered.

"A hundred matchmakers and their daughters have not, as yet, snared me into the parson's mousetrap."

He sounded inordinately proud of his achievement. Grudgingly Stacia supposed he was entitled to be, for as an excellent catch he must feel unrelenting pressure. It said much for his arrogance that he had been able to resist for all these years.

"I fancy you might be too much of a stickler to be pleased by any one female," she ventured, eyeing him sideways.

"I am the one who is found wanting, ma'am. Truth to tell, I am too fond of my bachelor freedoms to compromise them in marriage."

Stacia laughed, but there was a hollow sound to it. "I always understand that married gentlemen do continue to enjoy their bachelor freedoms."

"You have a jaundiced eye, Miss Gilbert," he teased, "which is remarkable in one so young."

"I have observed much," she confided, and he continued to look amused.

The phaeton turned into Tavistock Square, and knowing her acting was almost at an end, Stacia was almost regretful now. Her role was becoming unexpectedly enjoyable.

Suddenly his voice cut sharply into her pleasant thoughts as he brought the carriage to a halt outside her house. "I expect to be meeting Mr. Farramond for a game of piquet this evening. Shall I convey to him your good wishes?"

Her eyes narrowed suspiciously. "I cannot imag-

141

ine why you should think I would want you to, my lord."

He toyed with the buttons on his gloves. "I believed you and he had an accord."

"You are totally mistaken, Lord Silverwood," she told him, reverting to her cold demeanor. "Mr. Farramond is nothing to me, I assure you. One coze at a soiree does not signify an accord, or anything else."

"I confess I would have been surprised to hear you say anything else. The fellow's a gull-catcher, and not in the least timbered up to your weight."

"Indeed not," she responded with a grateful smile. "Only those up to the knocker are like to be found in my company. So," she ventured a moment later, "do you hope to fleece the fellow tonight?"

"Fleece him, Miss Gilbert?" the earl echoed in a disparaging tone. "I always play fair and square, but even if I did not, there would be little gain from Mr. Farramond; the clumperton does not wager sufficient to endure a grain of hardship."

Stacia drew a sigh of relief, for whatever grievance she felt at Damian's lack of support, she would not wish him to follow their father's road to ruin.

"How utterly unfashionable of him," she murmured.

He climbed down from the phaeton and came round to give her his hand while his tiger held the heads of the horses.

When she stepped down, the earl was slow in relinquishing her hand, saying, "This afternoon has been a delight, ma'am, more so for the unexpectedness of your condescension in accompanying me. My felicitations to Mrs. Copeland."

"And mine to Lady Charlotte." As he walked back to the phaeton, she added coyly, "I do hope we meet again before long."

He paused and subjected her to a lazy smile. "You can be absolutely sure that we will. Good day to you, ma'am."

Stacia waited outside the house until he had driven off, raising his whip to her in salute. As the phaeton disappeared around the corner, she sighed and was thoughtful, recalling as best she could all that had been said between them. All in all she was well pleased with the proceedings so far.

The first salvo in what might be a long campaign had been fired.

THIRTEEN

Lady Charlotte Fitch-Drummond sailed into the marble hallway of Silverwood House like a full-masted schooner in a gale and demanded to see her brother. Just as she did so, the earl came hurrying down the stairs.

"Lottie, my dear!" he greeted her. "What an unlooked-for surprise. What brings you here at this ungodly hour?"

Lady Charlotte eyed him shrewdly. "I was on my way to Shomberg House to select a few lengths of material for my new spring social calendar when I noticed your phaeton in the carriage drive. I've been wanting a coze with you for an age and deemed it provident to call in."

The earl eyed his sister indulgently as he asked in a lazy manner, "Did you not notice that your driver was taking you in the wrong direction for Shomberg House? You really must have words with him without delay."

Lady Charlotte gave him a wry smile. "Don't make dainty with me, Blaise. It is difficult enough to find an occasion of late when you are not attached to Miss Gilbert like a barnacle."

"Ah," the earl murmured, becoming suddenly enlightened. "You cannot blame that in me, my dear. Miss Gilbert is a delightful companion."

144

"So I supposed," his sister responded without enthusiasm.

A moment later, aware that the servants were listening intently to the conversation, Lord Silverwood ushered her across the hall. "Come into the study. I believe I can spare you a few moments of my time."

"That is most accommodating of you, dearest. I fancy your tailor can wait if my mantua-maker is able."

"Evidently you do not know Weston or you would not make bold statements of that sort," he answered dryly.

"Do not, I beg of you, apprise me of the iniquities of your tailor, Blaise. I hear it often enough from Ashley. Tailors and mantua-makers have more consequence than the most celebrated opera dancers."

After she had swept into the study and he closed the door, she said, "Your servants will only listen at the keyhole, Blaise, so this attempt at a private coze is to no avail."

"I know it, but one must go through the motions."

She sank down into a leather wing chair and began to strip off her gloves with deliberate precision. The earl ignored the various chairs and instead went over to the empty fireplace, placing one Hessian boot on the fender and staring into the sooty depths.

"Well, Lottie, what has brought you here in such a fidge this morning?"

She looked up in alarm. "Am I in a fidge?"

He turned to smile at her in an indulgent manner. "Yes, I suspect you are, especially if you have deigned to delay a shopping expedition, not to mention a visit to your mantua-maker. It sounds like serious business to me."

"Sarcasm is not called for, my dear," she retorted, and despite a censorious manner her features did soften a little. "Very well, I shall be blunt. It cannot have escaped anyone's notice that you and Miss Gilbert have been seen in each other's company often of late."

His expression didn't change one iota as he replied, "That should come as no surprise to you, Lottie. Everyone knows my predilection for actresses and opera dancers."

"She is very lovely, I own, and a successful actress to boot, exactly timbered up to your weight, Blaise. I should have been more surprised if you hadn't tried to make her your *chère amie.*"

"Lottie," he said quietly but nonetheless authoritatively, "allow me to make one thing absolutely clear to you: Miss Gilbert is no lightskirt."

"I would not wish to suggest that she is. She is perfectly sweet and charming, and even gives the appearance of being gently bred." At the obvious signs of her brother's irritation, she went on quickly, "Normally I would not deign to mention the matter; after all you are a grown man, and if you wish to take a *chère amie* or consort with cyprians, it is of no consequence to me."

"Precisely my sentiments, Lottie, so why do you insist upon wasting precious shopping time indulging in this coze with me?"

Lady Charlotte drew a small sigh, knowing that her brother's patience was not infinite. "Blaise, my dear, you are the last of the Silverwood line, and as you approach the age of thirty, you still have no heir."

146

At this point he came away from the fireplace and moved slowly toward the desk, where he began to toy with the quills and blotter. "Does that matter so much?"

"Indeed it does!"

"I don't think so, Lottie. I don't think it matters a jot."

"Stuff and nonsense! I am almost out of patience with you. You have restored respectability to the Silverwood title. It should be your wish to pass it on to your son. After all, you are nine and twenty."

"You do not need to remind me of that," he said, and then he added, looking up at her without feigning a fashionable boredom, "I have it in mind the name of Miss Seymour is about to be mentioned."

"I wouldn't presume to do any such thing, but you have your pick of young ladies each Season, all of whom are eligible and most willing to become Lady Silverwood. However, I doubt if that will always be so if you are known to have a *chère amie* set up in some house in Hampstead."

Lord Silverwood clucked his tongue with impatience. "Those cork-brained chits you would foist into my marriage bed would wish to become my countess if I possessed three heads and a hunchback."

"Don't be so certain. You might not always be first oars with eligible females, Blaise."

"That is of no account to me, and while we are harping on the subject, I should like you to make it absolutely clear to any of your cronies who chance to inquire: I have no intention of setting Miss Gilbert up in a house—in Hampstead or anywhere

147

else. Even if I were inclined to do so, let me assure you Miss Gilbert would not entertain the notion."

Lady Charlotte looked totally unbelieving. "Tush, Blaise! Every actress that ever trod the boards is seeking someone like you to set them up before their looks fade."

"My dear, I am not in the habit of explaining myself even to you. Suffice I will say, Miss Gilbert is charming company *and* at present the talk of the town, which in itself would be reason enough for me to seek her out, but she is also surprisingly naive for an actress. Perhaps she is more gently reared than anyone knows."

A further look of disbelief crossed his sister's face. "If I didn't know you better, I'd mistake you for a mooncalf."

"It's entirely possible you don't know me as well as you believe. *I* know that left to herself Miss Gilbert would be prey to every rake and scapegrace to cross her path."

Lady Charlotte began to get to her feet. "How gallant of you, my dear. That would be exceedingly moving testimony were you not a rake and occasionally a scapegrace, too. In any event I confess it is a relief to see Miss Tamassi less in evidence of late, but don't consider her to wear the willow for you. She has been seen in the company of Lowry Denman on more than one occasion."

"Even I do not pursue more than one lady of the theatrical fraternity at a time."

"If you insist upon being faithful to Miss Gilbert, you are like to set an entirely new fashion among Corinthians. Oh, by the by, Blaise, did you know that Miss Gilbert has let it be known she is seeking a house of her own and the new development in Hans Town has taken her fancy?"

Lord Silverwood hastened to usher her toward the door. "Miss Gilbert has certainly solicited my advice on the matter."

"Are you also aware it is generally held you will stump the blunt for the leasehold?"

Once again the earl looked bored. "I have no control over on-dits. The tattle-baskets will believe whatever they wish. I rely upon you to acquaint them with the truth."

"They will not believe me."

"Then they will be obliged to believe what is not true—as is usual."

When they reached the front door, Lady Charlotte paused to say, "When I attended Sally Jersey's breakfast the other day, one on-dit circulating had it that Miss Gilbert is in truth the daughter of a baronet, and I own it is an interesting theory."

In response to her interrogative look, the earl smiled genuinely for the first time since his sister had arrived. "Don't look to me for confirmation or denial, my love. I know all too well how the gabble-grinders—not that I regard you as such—enjoy their romantic stories far more than the mundane truth, which would not be received so eagerly."

"You are being exceedingly provoking, Blaise."

"So I am often told."

She cast him an exasperated look before standing on her toes to kiss his cheek. Then she became earnest once again. "Enough of funning; you know I only have your well-being at heart, don't you, dearest?"

He squeezed both her hands in his. "Have no

149

fears for me, Lottie. I am well able to take care of myself. Surely you know that."

"A fall is all the harder when it comes from a great height. Mayhap I should warn Miss Gilbert of that, too."

All at once his face grew dark. Lady Charlotte knew that look all too well. "Don't interfere, Lottie. I know what I am about."

His sister drew a deep sigh and nodded. "Have no fear," she whispered, touching his face briefly with her gloved hand before she hurried to her carriage. No sooner had it moved out into Park Lane than a tilbury pulled into the drive. Lord Silverwood bit back a gasp of exasperation when he recognized Damian Farramond sitting on the box.

The house steward glanced at his master, recognizing the signs. "Am I to say you are out, my lord?"

The earl hesitated, tempted by his servant's suggestion, but then he shook his head as Damian bounded up the steps.

"Lord Silverwood, what good fortune to find you at home. I had quite decided you would be out at this time."

The earl feigned a welcoming manner, saying, "Mr. Farramond, good morning to you, sir."

"My lord, I would be most obliged if you would give your expert eye to my new team."

The young man eyed the horses with both pride and hope while the earl surveyed them with disdain. Damian asked eagerly, "What do you think of them? Are they not a pair of prime bloods?"

Lord Silverwood did not give rein to his true opinion. He merely smiled, took up his whip from a stand near the door, and suggested, "Why don't we take a turn about the park, sir, so I may try them for myself?"

Damian Farramond's face was a picture of delight. "My lord! What condescension. What an honor that is. There is no greater dabster in the entire city of London, and I value no one's opinion more. Let us be gone with no further . . ."

Even as he spoke, making no effort to hide his gratitude or admiration for the earl, Lord Silverwood was sprinting down the steps toward the tilbury and pair, the gold tassels on his Hessian boots swinging as he went.

As Stacia awaited the earl's arrival with scarce-concealed impatience, she told herself it was only because her plan was proceeding so well. For all his superior airs his lordship was like so many other gentlemen who were easy prey for a calculating female.

On almost every afternoon when she was not required to rehearse, Lord Silverwood arrived in his high-perch phaeton to take her driving. Usually their destination was Hyde Park, but sometimes he drove her to Richmond Park, to Southwark, or to Vauxhall Gardens, which she found fascinating. Occasionally they visited Gunter's Tea Shop in Berkeley Square to enjoy their renowned ice creams, which Stacia loved. The earl appeared to find her pleasure in something he regarded as mundane amusing.

When the distinctive phaeton turned into the square, despite all her plans for his humiliation, Stacia couldn't prevent her heart from leaping. When she heard the maid admit him to the house, she went downstairs, wearing yet another new gown and

151

pelisse, these in cornflower blue. She saw the admiration in his eyes and knew it to be genuine. The plan was proceeding perfectly. He would soon be at her mercy and regarded as a bufflehead by all those who presently considered him bang up to the mark.

"Miss Gilbert," he greeted her with a warm smile that actually reached his eyes. "You present a delightful sight to someone who considered himself immune to female beauty."

She dimpled. "And I, my lord, am resistant to moonshine, so don't seek to pour the butterboat over me."

He laughed. "Your problem is having received far too much flummery of late."

"Is that possible?"

"Yes, if it means you are resistant to my flattery."

"Nothing could safeguard me from your Spanish coin, my lord."

"You once declared you were impervious to it."

Stacia lowered her lashes. "It was an untruth."

He escorted her out to the phaeton, but in the few minutes that had elapsed since his arrival, a shabby traveling carriage had drawn up behind it. Just as Lord Silverwood was about to hand Stacia up onto the box of the phaeton, a gentleman climbed down from the carriage and almost stumbled onto the pathway.

"It *is* you!" he called, waving his hand in her direction. "I thought it must be. You can't hoodwink me. Actress or not, I'd know you anywhere."

Both Stacia and Lord Silverwood turned around to face the newcomer, and she stiffened with alarm as Erasmus Chark lurched toward her, evidently the worse for drink but sober enough to spoil everything at such a crucial time. As the earl put himself between them, Mr. Chark pointed his finger at Stacia, who waited in fear to be revealed as Eustacia Farramond and have her carefully composed plan of revenge destroyed.

"What . . . what do you want with me?" she asked in an uneven voice.

His appearance was more unkempt than Stacia recalled, and it disgusted her as much as it had when her uncle suggested an alliance between them. That alone was sufficient reason for her to want to keep her distance.

"What do I want?" he echoed. "Our wedding, you silly widgeon, that is what I want. It's overdue, as you well know, and I'm an impatient bridegroom."

The earl stepped forward and said in a deceptively soft voice, "Whomever you are seeking, you are mistaken in believing it to be this lady, sir. Be pleased to remove yourself, after tendering an apology for the intrusion, naturally."

"You can whistle for your apology and I shan't go without m'bride," the old man declared, "even if some man-milliner says I should."

If the situation hadn't been so fraught, Stacia might have been amused to hear the earl being so described, but in truth she was terrified of discovery, and that was uppermost in her mind.

"The chit's promised to me," Mr. Chark insisted, and despite his being deep in his cups, Stacia was afraid the earl would believe him. "I'll sue her for breach of promise, that's what I'll do, or my name isn't Erasmus Chark."

Lord Silverwood moved toward him, but drink had made Mr. Chark bold and he was not intimidated. The earl took him by his arm and drew him

153

unwillingly toward his carriage. "Mr. Chark," he said in a reasonable tone, "Miss Gilbert is nothing to you, now or in the future."

"I won't be slumguzzled by some town spark—"

"Listen to me carefully, sir," the earl entreated. "You will get back into your carriage *now*. . . ."

The fellow attempted to extricate himself from the earl's grip to no avail. "This is out of all bounds, sir!" he protested.

"My feelings precisely."

Mr. Chark almost danced back to his carriage, so swiftly did the earl propel him along the pavement. "Look here," the fellow protested, "the law's on my side, I'll have you know."

When they'd reached the carriage, the earl said—and foxed or not, Mr. Chark could not possibly mistake the menace in his voice—"If you know what is best for your continuing good health, sir, you will go with no more ado and not seek to contact Miss Gilbert in person or by communication ever again."

"You can't do this!" Mr. Chark protested as he was thrust none too kindly into his carriage.

"Yes, I can, and let me assure you, if Miss Gilbert informs me that you have at any time tried to contact her, I shall seek you out and give you a good basting."

"This is an outrage!" came the lame protest from inside the carriage.

"Outrage or not, do you understand what I am telling you, sir?" the earl asked in a voice of steel.

"What the deuce? That bit of muslin was always a branding iron. She's yours, sir, and welcome. She's out of all nick and she'll cut your comb, just you wait and see."

Lord Silverwood looked grim as he brought his

whip down on the leader of the team, and the carriage jerked into motion. Feeling profound dismay, Stacia watched it go and saw Mr. Chark's red face at the window before the carriage moved out of sight. As the earl came back toward her, she didn't know whether to laugh or to cry.

"I don't belive that jug-bitten fellow will trouble you again, ma'am," he remarked, and she was amazed at his equilibrium in the face of such a to-do.

In spite of her own tumultuous emotions, she averted her eyes and said, "I am truly indebted to you, my lord."

His expression softened as he looked down on her. "This is one of the less-attractive aspects of achieving fame, my dear. Zanies are drawn to those who attain renown. It isn't a pleasant prospect, but it is like to happen. You must try not to let it disconcert you more than is necessary. Before long you will have grown quite used to it happening."

Stacia made a heroic effort to regain her composure. At least she had not been shown up for a sham in front of his lordship. If Erasmus Chark was to accost her again, she could only hope it was in private, but she was certain the earl's warning would frighten him away for good. For all his bluster he was not a brave man, and the earl, as Stacia had once surmised, was a formidable adversary. Mr. Chark could not help but appreciate it.

She contrived to give him a tremulous smile. "I doubt that I could ever grow used to situations such as that, but if, in the future, some bosky old quiz accosts me in the street, I can only hope you are present to protect me and deal with him as magnificently as you did just now."

As he handed her belatedly onto the box, he replied, "That is my wish, too, Miss Gilbert. I hope it will always be my honor to serve you."

FOURTEEN

"I am persuaded that *Venice Preserved* will be your greatest triumph," Mr. Allbury told Stacia as she left the stage after a dress rehearsal of the taxing role.

"She is going to be the greatest Belvidera who ever stepped onto a stage," Paris Kingswell added.

Stacia's cheeks colored at their praise. "Thank you, gentlemen. Your faith in me is most heartening, but let us first await the critical acclaim before crying roast meat."

"Your acclaim is a foregone conclusion," Mr. Kingswell declared.

"We're sold out for the first night," Mr. Allbury told her as he rushed off to check the receipts for the following night.

"There is no stopping us now," Mr. Kingswell confided, unable to hide his excitement. When they began to walk toward their dressing rooms, he went on, "We could, in fact, become even greater if we were known as a couple—in real life as well as on the stage."

For a moment Stacia appeared bewildered, and then she laughed. "Paris, what a strange proposal. I'm persuaded you cannot possibly be in earnest."

"I have never been more in earnest, my dear. You must surely be aware of my great regard for you."

Her face relaxed into an indulgent smile. "I am greatly honored by your proposal, Paris, and equally fond of you, but not sufficient to marry you."

The actor looked crestfallen. "I feared as much, my dear. Had you accepted me I would have been the happiest of men, but I recognize that Lord Silverwood plays a great part in your life nowadays, and he is the greatest competition for any man."

"It has nothing to do with Lord Silverwood, Paris. Not in the least," she hastened to assure him. "My answer would have been exactly the same had I never met his lordship."

Paris Kingswell appeared somewhat astonished at her confession. "I don't challenge your ... er ... affection for the gentleman, but you must be mindful of the fact that he cannot offer you marriage."

"Nor do I seek such an offer," she hastened to explain. "Let me assure you, despite outward appearances, Lord Silverwood and I are merely acquaintances. My being seen with the most sought-after beau in the ton is good for me as an actress, and he, in his turn, has his reputation as a nonesuch enhanced by my hanging on to his arm. There is nothing more to the matter than that."

Paris Kingswell looked startled by her candor, and she quickly added, "You really are very dear to me, Paris, but not sufficient to accept your offer, which is most appreciated, I assure you."

"I don't intend to withdraw it. I wish it to stand, and should you change your mind at any time, you only have to tell me. I still believe we could make a wonderful match."

When Stacia returned to her dressing room, she

was choked with emotion. The offer of marriage was as moving as it was unexpected. So much that had happened of late was unexpected, from her success at the Regency, her popularity in fashionable circles, to the unexpected matter of enjoying Lord Silverwood's company.

On any of the many occasions she had been in his company of late, he had shown himself to be both charming and amiable, able to make her laugh with a clever turn of phrase and divert her with a witty anecdote. Often when she had returned from the theater, exhausted, he had displayed the greatest concern for her, while never on one occasion overstepping the bounds of propriety. He had at every turn ensured they were properly chaperoned, and all Stacia's carefully rehearsed put-downs were never uttered.

Lately she and the earl had been seen everywhere together, in his phaeton and on his arm. There could be no member of the beau monde who did not know they were keeping company, and all were bound to assume they shared the closest relationship. It had gone just as she had planned, save for the unexpected discovery that she could actually enjoy his company, a minor deviation to the original design that would not be allowed to spoil the outcome of her purpose.

Once the purchase of her house was completed, she was aware the time would have arrived for her to drop him in the most conspicuous manner.

It suited her that her much-vaunted search for a house of her own in the little village of Knight's Bridge was considered a gift from the besotted earl by those who regarded themselves as well informed. When she was settled in, her intention was

159

to take up in the most public manner with another of the bucks who was in pursuit of her, leaving Lord Silverwood with his shattered pride to face the laughter of his peers.

However, as that time grew near, Stacia was becoming less enthusiastic about her objective. If she left it too long to act upon the final—most important—part of the plan, then it was likely the earl would tire of her and take up with another, and Stacia would find herself in the position she had chosen for him to occupy.

"My dear, you look totally hag-ridden," Maura declared when Stacia returned to the dressing room. "Mr. Allbury is driving you too hard. Tackling all these diverse roles is taxing, even for one with your stamina."

"No, 'tis nothing," Stacia protested. "The role is demanding, but I am equal to it, and as you are aware, I enjoy a diversity of parts."

"That is only because you possess a remarkable memory for lines. Your power has grown apace since you came to London."

As Stacia sank down onto a little boudoir chair, she asked, "Then why do I feel such dissatisfaction?"

"Like most artists, you seek perfection and, mayhap, feel you can never attain it."

"No, it isn't that, Maura. I do as well as I am able, and it appears to please. It is more than I ever expected."

"If it is any consolation, I believe you *have* attained perfection."

Stacia smiled, albeit halfheartedly. "You are far too indulgent of me."

"I am truthful. Surely your unease doesn't stem

from a fear that Mr. Chark will seek you out again." (Stacia had reported the incident to Maura.)

The notion made Stacia laugh. "Indeed I am not. His lordship dealt with that gentleman most efficiently."

"How I wish I had been able to witness it."

"So do I. Now I can be amused by what happened, but at the time I was put out of countenance, I assure you."

"Humdudgeon causes so many problems."

Stacia chose to ignore the reference to her double life and confided, "Seeing Mr. Chark made me more than ever glad I absconded from my uncle's care. Damian consoled me at the time with the possibility I should soon be left a wealthy widow. I am delighted to see Mr. Chark is still in good heart but even happier I have been gone for more than six years!"

Maura chuckled, but then she hesitated before asking, "How goes it with his lordship?"

Startled, Stacia looked up wide-eyed. "As well as possible."

"To anyone who sees you in his company, it would appear you enjoy a fond relationship."

"That is what I intended."

"The appearance seems to be so genuine, I've been wondering if you had experienced a change of heart since coming to know him better."

"If I am to be lauded as an actress, I may as well put my talent to good use."

"Then it is certain you have achieved perfection." Maura hesitated once again before she asked, "Does it not trouble you to consider that his lordship might have grown genuinely fond of you?"

Stacia laughed harshly. "Maura! What nonsense you speak. His pride was injured—mortally, no doubt—when I first gave him the go-by. This is his way of redeeming himself in front of his cronies. As soon as the next fashionable takes, I shall have my turnips. What Lord Silverwood does not appreciate is that he is about to receive *his*."

"Forgive me for saying this, Stacia, but from all I have observed, hatred often feeds on the host, not the object."

Before Stacia could answer, there came a light knock on the door. When Maura went to answer it, she stepped back to allow Damian Farramond to enter. Immediately Stacia jumped to her feet, and Maura, after glancing curiously at the visitor, excused herself, leaving them alone.

"Damian! I did not look to see you again after our last encounter."

He stood before her, fingering his hat and looking awkward. The points of his shirt collar were so stiff and high, she thought he looked slightly ridiculous, making it uncomfortable for him to turn his head, unlike Lord Silverwood, who always dressed to perfection.

"Nor did I," he confessed, glancing around her dressing room as if embarrassed to be there.

"Am I no longer a disgrace to you?" she asked, more sharply than she intended when she came to acknowledge she was comparing every gentleman she encountered of late unfavorably with the earl.

When he didn't reply, she went on, making no pretense at hiding her bitterness. "How odd it is that elevated society makes much of me and yet you are ashamed. You're not in the least ashamed

162

to visit the theater and to enjoy the performance. How bizarre that is."

Her brother's cheeks grew a little redder than usual as he replied, "Don't put the bridle on the wrong horse, Eustacia. It was not I who ran away and became embroiled in this kind of life."

"I had good reason to do so, as you well know. However, I am too fatigued just now to break straws with you. What brings you here? Surely not solely out of concern for my well-being, for as you can observe, I am doing very well indeed."

Damian looked all the more discomfited. "A few days ago I received a visit from Erasmus Chark, who had heard of your newfound fame and wished, understandably, to reacquaint himself with you."

She groaned softly. "Am I to assume it was you who gave him my direction?"

Her brother looked abashed. "He was making such a to-do, I was obliged to tell him lest he disturb Peg with his bellowing. I deemed you fit enough to face him out."

"You are all consideration," Stacia responded, and he was bound to be aware of the heavy irony in her voice. "I trust your wife and family are well despite their vexations."

"The children are in the pink of health, I thank you, although Peggy, I regret to say, is sorely afflicted at present with an attack of the vapors."

"I am truly sorry to hear you say so," Stacia told him, although she suspected her brother's wife might be prone to frequent attacks of a nervous nature.

"She heard recently that Lord Silverwood was about to set you up in a house as his . . ."

As Damian floundered about in search of the

163

least indelicate word, Stacia mercilessly scoffed, "His what, Damian? His lightskirt? Paphian? Demirep? Doxy, perhaps? Ah, yes, doxy it is. Respectable females do not take to the boards, so why does my personal life disturb you so? Is it not only what you might expect of me?"

His face grew even more ruddy. "My stars! Your life of disrepute has made you coarse, Eustacia. No wonder poor Peggy was knocked off her hinges by our connection. You cannot blame it in her."

"You can tell poor Peg that when my house is purchased, as it will be very soon, its cost will be borne by me. I am no one's convenient."

"Even if that were true, it makes no odds, for no one will believe it."

"I don't care a fig for what anyone else believes!"

His eyes suddenly filled with fury. "Then have a thought for those who do!"

"I recall a time when few people cared about *my* feelings, Damian."

"So this is to be your revenge, is it?"

"Not upon you and your wife, you may be sure."

"How can I be? You are seen all around town with the fellow. Lord Silverwood, of all people. Do you have no recollection of the name?"

Her eyes narrowed. "I thought it was you who might have forgotten. I certainly have not, but you seem to have a liking for hanging on to his lordship's coattails. You even sit down to gamble with him. After Father's fate, I don't know how you could."

The young man began to bluster, "Dash it all, Eustacia. You know as well as I, being seen with Blaise Silverwood is a great elevation. In most ways he's a first-rater, and as for gaming with the fellow, I am not a rip-rascal like Father. The circumstances are quite different."

"My mistake," she answered. "I rather fancy your wife puts a check string on your purse, so you couldn't possibly game too deep even if you were inclined to do so." Her brother's cheeks colored up, and Stacia immediately regretted her waspishness. "I beg your pardon, Damian. That comment was totally uncalled for."

The young man pulled at his waistcoat. "Despite the fact we always seem to break straws when we meet, I have no wish for us to part brass rags. Will you not reconsider my offer of a home beneath our roof, Eustacia?" he asked in a piteous tone. "It is still not too late for your redemption."

Unexpectedly for Mr. Farramond, who became startled, Stacia began to laugh. "I am exceedingly grateful to you, Damian, for the offer, but you may be assured I have no intention of giving up my independence, nor, you can inform your wife, have I in any way become allied to the Earl of Silverwood. I hope the knowledge will save her maidservant from being obliged to burn feathers next time I am seen in his company. Now I must ask you to leave so I'm able to take my rest."

After he had opened the dressing-room door, he paused as if about to say something else. Then, after a moment, he murmured, "How different life could have been for us."

"Not for you, Damian. For me, I daresay, but I do the best I can with the cards dealt me. That is all anyone can possibly do."

"Truth to tell, Eustacia, I admire you. Truly I do. I would not have had the courage. I just hope you understand the difficulty of my position."

165

She went up to him and put her hand on his arm in a gesture of sympathy, just as Lord Silverwood came to a standstill a few yards away from them in the corridor. Abruptly Stacia drew her hand away. Damian nodded to both of them, and then, replacing his hat at what he obviously considered a jaunty angle, he rushed out of the theater.

"What did *he* want?" the earl asked as he frowned after the departing figure.

Stacia took a moment to compose herself before replying, a little breathlessly, "He just wished to convey his felicitation to me."

"The fellow's a prosy bore," the earl told her as he came into the dressing room and closed the door behind him. "I hope you've sent him away with a flea in his ear."

Stacia bit back her annoyance at having her brother so portrayed, even if the description was an accurate one.

"If I am weary, it's because the role I'm presently rehearsing is a most taxing one, but," she added, casting him a conciliatory smile, "receiving a visit from you is bound to refresh me."

He returned her smile and then tossed his hat onto the dressing table suddenly, causing her heart to constrict. What was happening to her? she asked herself in dismay, and she knew just then that she must end the farce soon or suffer unwanted consequences.

The visit from her brother, Paris Kingswell's unexpected proposal of marriage, her sudden success in London, and now these strange ambivalent feelings about Lord Silverwood conspired to put her head in a spin. She bit her lip as tears came unbidden to her eyes, and suddenly the earl was all concern for her.

"My dear Stacia, what is amiss? That widgeon has put you out of sorts, hasn't he?" When she shook her head, he said grimly, "I believe I will be obliged to have serious words with Mr. Allbury. He is driving you too hard."

"I drive myself hard. Did you not realize?"

"Then it will have to stop. I insist that you rest for a while immediately. I shall leave and let you sleep for a spell."

"Oh, no . . ." she began to protest.

"I have no intention of allowing you to become ill."

He reached out to brush away a solitary tear that had spilled onto her cheek, and the tenderness in his voice and manner toward her made her want to run away. When he began to lead her to the daybed, the air between them seemed suddenly charged. In her state of heightened emotion Stacia was more aware of him than ever before, and that feeling quickly transferred itself to him. After casting her a curious glance, he drew her closer to him.

"Stacia," he murmured, gently caressing her neck, and she trembled slightly at his touch, aware of the strength of the arms that were about her.

She had never forgotten what it was like to be held by him, not for a single moment. This time she went eagerly into his arms without any of the guile she normally engaged when in his company. Quite simply what she wanted was to be surrounded by his strength, something that excluded the rest of the world.

She looked up at him, into his dark, fathomless eyes, which usually revealed nothing, only now

167

they reflected her own desire. Her lips met his with an abandon she might once have thought shameful, and the effect upon her emotions was just as devastating as on that other occasion. Only his cruelty and disdain were absent, although the passion remained and was perhaps even greater than before.

"Just as you warned me," she whispered against his lips, "I am humbled."

He laughed softly and replied, "You are not humbled; you are glorious, and I intend to make you mine."

So saying, he took her into his arms once again, where she wished she could stay for evermore.

FIFTEEN

"Oh, give me daggers, fire, or water.
How I could bleed, how burn,
how drown the wave,
huzzing and foaming around my sinking head."

The audience was totally engrossed in Stacia's performance, hanging on to every word of her demented heroine as she verged on madness. The auditorium was both crowded and hushed, an unusual combination. Rarely did silence reign in both the pit and the gallery. Those who normally visited a theater merely to harangue the actors attended her every word on this occasion.

Prudently Lord Silverwood had engaged the box nearest the stage, which he shared with Lady Charlotte, her husband, Captain Fielding and his wife, and Sir Hubert Patch, who never failed to deliver flowers to Stacia's dressing room on every first night, although he had long since given up any hope of finding favor.

He leaned close to the earl and whispered, "Good grief, Sil, the chit's magnificent, is she not? I'd better make myself amiable to her for when you tire of her company."

"She is surpassing herself," Lady Charlotte whispered to her brother from behind her fan. "There is

169

a new depth to her acting I had never noted before."

His lordship didn't reply, for he was too intent upon following every moment Stacia was on the stage. His sister noted his intense interest and sighed.

"If only Miss Gilbert were highborn, she would be perfect for you."

Stacia hazarded a brief glance toward the box where she knew the earl would be ensconced. He smiled faintly in her direction so as not to put her off her stride. The sight of him did affect her, she was bound to admit.

> *"Hell! Hell! Burst from the center of rage and roar aloud. If they art half so hot, so mad as I am murmuring streams, soft shades, and spring flowers! Lutes, laurels, seas of milk, and ships of amber."*

The acting was automatic, as was her recital of the words. Her thoughts were wholly of Lord Silverwood, and she knew just then with absolute certainty what a fool she had been to believe she had hated him. She had never hated him. From the moment she had set eyes upon him as a child, she had not hated him. Her passion sprang forth from the other end of the emotional spectrum.

What a foolish notion it had been to believe she could bring him down among his acquaintances. He would not be humiliated by her, as she had so gleefully planned. She had become the fool, not he. It was she who was at his mercy, not the other way around, for very soon she would no longer be able to resist the temptation of his embrace, and then she would be no more than a prisoner to his bidding, living only for the time spent in his company.

Because Stacia paused far longer than supposed, the prompter whispered, *"Farewell"* from the wings, and Stacia tottered back, her hand to her head, only this was not acting. Her anguish was all too real. Her legs had grown weak with the enormity of comprehending at last the irony of her situation. The truth she was now forced to confront caused her to stumble against the foot lamps. Instantly she flinched away, but not quickly enough, and some members of the audience and cast gasped as a spark of flame ignited the hem of her gown.

Gazing at it in horror, Stacia screamed as the flimsy muslin material caught light. Before anyone else had the foresight to act, the earl jumped up from his seat, climbed over the side of the box, slid down onto the stage, and raced across the apron, stripping off his evening coat as he ran.

When he reached her, she was screaming in terror, beating against the skirt of her gown helplessly. With little finesse he pushed her to the ground, at the same time stifling the flames with his coat. Shock had rendered Stacia suddenly silent, although a wave of dismay spread among the audience, which began to strain forward to gain a better view of the calamity.

"Does it hurt very much?" the earl asked tersely.

All at once Stacia became aware of the agonizing pain, and her head swam alarmingly. By this time the stage had begun to fill, and the audience, more than ever anxious for a better view of the proceedings, crushed forward against the stage. Stacia was aware of a sea of faces around her, but the only one of importance was Lord Silverwood, who had, she realized, saved her life.

"Fetch cold water and bandages, Lottie," he ordered.

Even while swooning, Stacia was amazed to see Lady Charlotte tearing off a strip of her own petticoat, not caring who saw her do so, while her brother frantically pulled away the charred part of Stacia's own gown to reveal the reddened flesh beneath.

Mr. Allbury was wringing his hands in anguish as he stood over his stricken protégée. "This is catastrophic!" he wailed. "My theater could have burned down."

Paris Kingswell cast him a disgusted look. "It might as well burn down if you lose your finest actress, for it would be little use to you without her."

Lady Charlotte returned with a bowl of water and dipped her torn petticoat into it. When Lord Silverwood wrapped the soaked cloth around Stacia's scorched legs, she cried out in pain.

"It's necessary," he told her. "Hold hard there, my love."

My love. Stacia's head dropped back, and tears slid down her cheeks. Anyone who saw them would mistake them for tears of pain, which they were. Only the pain in her heart was far greater than those of her burns, which would, no doubt, heal in due course.

"Bring her some laudanum," the earl demanded, looking around in desperation. "For pity's sake, can't one of you find it somewhere?"

Moments later a vial was produced, and Lady Charlotte administered a few drops to Stacia, who did not refuse the palliative. "You are being very brave, my dear," her ladyship murmured, a comment that caused Stacia's tears to flow again, but the laudanum soon began to have its effect, and the pain was becoming dull.

"The carriage has been brought round," she heard someone say.

"We'll soon have you as right as a trivet," the earl told her as he lifted her very gently into his arms, but the pitying look on his face gave lie to his optimism.

"No one is ever all bad or all good," she murmured sleepily as she laid her head against his shoulder.

For the moment she could allow herself the luxury of being close to him, something she was aware she would not enjoy for much longer.

"What did she say?" Lady Charlotte asked.

"The laudanum's making her squiffy," her brother told her.

Stacia's head nestled comfortably against the earl's broad shoulders, and that was her last recollection of that awful evening before she lapsed finally into a state of total unconsciousness.

When she awoke, it was to find herself in a strange bed in an unfamiliar room, wearing a night shift that was not her own. Although heavy velvet curtains were drawn across the windows, she was aware there was daylight beyond them.

As she came back to consciousness, Stacia must have made some sound, for a woman who'd been sitting in the corner stood up and approached the bed.

"Where am I?" Stacia asked, dreading to discover she was in Silverwood House.

"I am Lady Charlotte's housekeeper, ma'am. Mrs. Curley's the name. Her ladyship has charged me with the task of caring for you until you feel less poorly, although Mrs. Copeland has taken her turn. She's gone home to change her clothes and will return to see you presently."

"So this is Lady Charlotte's house."

"Yes, ma'am."

"How kind of her to accommodate me. How long . . . ?"

"Two nights since you were brought in, ma'am. You've slept a good deal. Dr. Shilton thought it best, so he prescribed a sleeping draft for you."

Stacia had a vague recollection of being handled into bed and being bathed, and of hushed voices all around her. Now as she came back to full consciousness, she became aware of her legs, which were unbelievably sore. Before she could ask Mrs. Curley of their condition, the bedroom door opened and Lady Charlotte entered, accompanied by a tall, distinguished-looking gentleman.

"Dr. Shilton hoped you'd be awake for this visit," Lady Charlotte told her as she approached the bed. "How do you feel this morning?"

"Sore."

"That is entirely understandable," Dr. Shilton declared as he put his bag down on the night table. "You are an exceedingly fortunate young lady, allow me to inform you. Lady Charlotte explained his lordship's prompt action to me, and I applauded him. Now let us see the damage."

When the covers were drawn back, Stacia could see that Lady Charlotte's tattered petticoat had been replaced by clean, neat bandages.

174

As Dr. Shilton began to unwind them, she asked, "Are my legs scarred?"

"It's difficult to say at this stage, Miss Gilbert," the doctor replied, "but due to his lordship's prompt action I believe the damage will be minimal, although you might not credit it now."

His prognosis came as a relief, and she sank back into the pillows until the bandages were totally removed, and then she dared to look at the injury for herself. The scorched skin was beginning to peel to reveal angry flesh beneath. The sight of her legs made her wince. It was just as Dr. Shilton had told her—it was hard to believe she would not be left scarred.

"There is no infection, which is an excellent sign," the doctor explained a moment later, and then, when he applied a healing salve, Stacia was obliged to grit her teeth.

Finally new bandages were wrapped around the affected parts, and it was a great relief to the patient when he was finished and Mrs. Curley tidied the bed.

"I shall call in upon you on the morrow," Dr. Shilton promised, and then, as he glanced around the room, said, "I confess I have never seen such a colorful sickroom." She smiled as he added, "I have a vested interest in restoring you completely to health, Miss Gilbert. Since you came to town, I have very much enjoyed your performances at the Regency and look forward to doing so again in the very near future."

"Not so close to the foot lamps in future, though," she managed to respond.

They all laughed, and before he departed he

added, "I believe some sustenance is now in order. You must begin to rebuild your strength."

Lady Charlotte escorted the physician out of the room, and Mrs. Curley bustled away to fetch the beef tea that had been prescribed. Stacia, however, was not left alone for long before Maura returned from Tavistock Square.

"Lady Charlotte told me you had regained your senses, dearest. What a relief that is to me. How do you feel?"

"Grateful. Grateful to all those who are being so kind, and especially to his lordship for his prompt action."

"I am bound to own he was quite magnificent. Lady Charlotte says there is talk of nothing else wherever she goes, and for the first time in both their lives she is inordinately proud of her brother."

"I shall never forget it, but what a clunch I am to do such a foolish thing, Maura. How could I have been so careless?"

"It wasn't your fault."

"Everyone is fully aware of the import of keeping well away from any of the lamps. It was one of the first things I learned."

"You were evidently caught up in the drama of your role."

Stacia was glad enough to allow the credibility of that belief. As she watched Maura bring out a selection of books, her favorite cologne, combs, brushes, and even some lip rouge, she sank back into the pillows once again, reflecting that her injuries notwithstanding it was good to have nothing to do for once and for others to fuss over her. She couldn't recall when it had happened before. Perhaps in the long-forgotten days of her early childhood before Lord Silverwood's gaming had ruined them. For the first time, though, she considered it might have been more her father's fault than that of the earl. Devin Farramond had been a weak man and easily tempted by the green baize of the gaming tables, but she could not, however much she wished to do so, mitigate the earl's part in their downfall. He had taken advantage of her father's weakness. Even at so young an age he must have been shrewd enough to know he was taking on a habitual loser in gaming matters.

"Have you seen anything of his lordship?" Stacia couldn't stop herself from asking.

Maura had been busy putting a change of nightclothes in the dresser. "He has scarce been off the doorstep since he brought you here that night. My goodness, Stacia, he's been as fussy as a hen with only the one chick!"

Recollections of being swept up into his strong arms remained her abiding memory of that disastrous evening. Even the pain she had suffered, then as now, was surpassed by that particular recollection.

"As soon as you are well enough, he is bound to visit you. I gained the distinct impression he was merely kicking his heels until you were well enough to receive him." Stacia sighed profoundly, and her friend inquired, "Why so Friday-faced, my love? There is not one of us who has met him who wouldn't wish to be the object of his admiration. He has every appearance of a man lost for love. Is that not what you wished?"

"It was what I planned, but it is all such a hum, Maura. I have attempted to come the artful with

177

him, but I am the one left in the hips, and you are like to say it is no more than I deserve."

"I certainly wouldn't dream of saying such a thing to you." As she began to smooth out the counterpane, Maura added, "I'm persuaded you're being unnecessarily blue-deviled, my dear, due in part, I have no doubt, to the drafts Dr. Shilton has obliged you to consume. You'll soon be as pert as a pearmonger again."

"I fear I will not."

"When you are somewhat more recovered and not in so much discomfort, you will be in great spout again."

"I doubt it."

Maura frowned. "I have always sensed there was something more to your relationship with his lordship than a simple dislike of his arrogance, as you have always led me to believe. Did you happen to know him before you joined the troupe?"

Once again the invalid sighed, and then she began to relate the entire story to her friend. "Papa was such a dear man, save for his weaknesses, that I'd far rather blame his lordship for our downfall," she told Maura at the end of her tale.

"What a dreadful experience for you at so tender an age," she gasped when Stacia had finished. "And as for Lord Silverwood, now you are famous and will never want again, it wouldn't matter a jot, would it not, except you have been foolish enough to fall under his spell?"

"What an imbecile I am."

"So are we all when it comes to love. If you are seeking my counsel, then I advise you to tell Lord Silverwood all. Confess who you are, and then you will be able to start afresh."

178

Stacia cast her a sharp look. "I cannot possibly do so, Maura. Imagine how he would look upon me if I were to tell him that on all our encounters of late my flirting and conversation were all a sham, maintained only for the vile purpose of punishing him for something that happened so many years ago, he's probably forgotten all about it."

"It wasn't a sham," Maura pointed out, "whatever your original intention."

"How can I confess that I have loathed him for more than half my life and I have schemed in order to humiliate him?" Stacia went on as if her friend had not spoken.

"But you haven't humiliated him. You have done nothing as yet."

"It is all the same. If I could forget all the unhappiness of the past, the fact remains I am an actress and all his solicitous attention has been aimed at seduction. I am not willing to be his bit of muslin, even if that means I am never to clap eyes upon him again."

Just as the words were spoken, Stacia found that possibility unbearable. Never to see his smile, feel the strength of his arms around her. The possibility was worse than anything that had gone before, but throughout those years of hardship she had contrived to retain her pride, and she was not willing to give it up now.

"He may not have a fancy for the Honorable Blanche Seymour, but she is precisely the kind of whey-faced chit he will eventually make his countess."

Their conversation was brought to an abrupt halt by the return of Mrs. Curley with the beef tea.

"I must beg your pardon for causing you so much extra work, Mrs. Curley," Stacia told her.

"Not at all, ma'am. I've quite enjoyed the change in our staid routine."

Despite her lack of appetite Stacia contrived to take some of the beef tea and afterward felt tiredness encroach. It was to be the pattern of the following few days until Dr. Shilton declared her sufficiently recovered to leave her bed. The bottom half of her legs remained an ugly mass of scorched flesh, but the pain had lessened, and she took comfort in the fact that if scars remained, her skirts would hide them.

It was now possible for her to join Lady Charlotte and her family for dinner, but Stacia feigned weakness and remained in her bedchamber. She dreaded being in the earl's company again. The knowledge that he called in often to inquire of her only added to her anguish.

When she got up from her sickbed, a trickle of visitors was allowed in when they called. Apart from Lady Charlotte, who had been a frequent caller from the outset, first to arrive after kicking his heels for several days was Paris Kingswell, bearing so many flowers, he could scarcely carry them.

"Good grief!" Stacia cried when she saw them. "You have already sent sufficient flowers to fill a florist's shop."

"These were merely those left at the theater today," he explained, handing them to Maura, who went to find vases.

"Poor Lady Charlotte," Stacia murmured, "she will not have a vase left in her entire house. This is

180

a fine pickle," she greeted him wryly after he had divested himself of the flowers.

"The matter of the greatest import is that of your recovery."

"That is well in hand," she assured him, turning away in some embarrassment.

Ever since he had made his offer of marriage, she had begun to feel awkward in his company. Since admitting to herself where her true affections belonged, she experienced even greater embarrassment in his presence.

"You look magnificent," he told her. "No one would ever know you'd suffered such terrible injuries only a short time ago."

"If that is so, it can only be because I have received the best treatment possible."

"So you should, as the greatest actress currently on the London stage. Only the very best of everything will do for you, my dear."

Her pale cheeks grew pink at such fulsome praise. "That, I think, is doing it too brown."

"You are also the most modest actress on the London stage. It is almost an unknown quality." He drew a sigh. "How I would wish to be Lord Silverwood in the service he did you." When she made no response, he went on, "Loath as I am to say it, I believe his devotion must go far beyond what anyone could reasonably expect."

"You may be sure I am exceedingly grateful to him, Paris."

"It is quite ironic, I feel, that whereas I am often called upon to play the hero, his lordship was actually able to be one. His actions were truly heroic. Now it is like I shall never have a chance to win your heart."

181

"You never did, my dear," she told him.

"I did have my hopes, and I have no intention of abandoning them entirely."

Stacia cast him a shrewd look. "It is well known, is it not, that gentlemen of Lord Silverwood's standing are rarely constant to ladies of my calling."

Paris Kingswell's face was covered in confusion. "My dear girl, I implied no such thing."

"Don't fret," she begged him. "I have no hopes in that direction."

Looking somewhat relieved, the actor got to his feet, saying hastily, "I won't remain any longer. Lady Charlotte issued a stern warning not to tire you, and as I am somewhat in awe of her, I intend to obey. Everyone at the theater sends their fondest regards to you and will, naturally, call upon you themselves in due course. You must contrive to hurry back to us, for you are sorely missed."

His sincerity couldn't be doubted, and she was moved by it. "Dear Paris," she said in a choked voice as she clasped his hands in hers.

There was scarcely time for her to wipe away a tear before another visitor was ushered in, this time Thomas Allbury. Maura, who had returned with several vases, was arranging the flowers in them, and she made a wry face when the manager was shown in.

"My dear Stacia," he greeted her heartily. "Mrs. Copeland. How well you are caring for our precious asset."

"I have long regarded her as a dear friend," Maura told him when she returned to her task.

Momentarily Mr. Allbury looked discomfited. "Quite so," he murmured, and then returned his attention to his protégée. "How pale you look. What a calamity. I do trust you are once again up to the knocker."

"Very nearly, sir," she assured him, and then added, "I am truly sorry for what happened."

"You were not in the least to blame for it. It could happen to anyone, I daresay, and due to Lord Silverwood's prompt action both you *and* the theater were saved. I recall very well watching Drury Lane burn down not so many years ago, and Covent Garden not much later than that, so it was not such an edifying thought that it could happen to *mine*. Let us speak of happier matters. I have brought the text of a new play for you, my dear, the promised comedy. I believe it will help you to while away your convalescence if you have lines to learn."

"That is very thoughtful of you, sir, but even the great Sarah Siddons couldn't play comedy."

"You are not the divine Sarah. You have the potential to be greater, given time and maturity."

"You credit me with a talent I may not possess."

"I am the manager, my dear. Allow me to decide. You are my greatest attraction, but we have maintained satisfactory houses since you were injured only because there are those ghouls who wanted to see where Stacia Gilbert almost burned to death, not a desire to see other actresses perform in your stead." When she shuddered, he went on quickly, "You may be sure I have penned a note to Lord Silverwood indicating how obliged I am for his heroism."

"No more than I, I assure you," Stacia told him, her tone ironic.

"Oh, indeed, and so you should be." And then he went on, "Time presses, my dear. I must be away to

183

attend to my business. Not all my actresses are as professional as you in needing little supervision. Always pulling caps and flying up onto the high ropes, so I am obliged to be vigilant. If only they were all like you, I would be a far happier and more wealthy man."

"He does not intend you to be idle even when you are so severely indisposed," Maura pointed out when he had gone.

"I wouldn't be in the least surprised to hear he'd been selling scraps of my burned clothing, but I cannot hold him in dislike. I owe him a good deal for my current success."

"Your success is due in no small measure to your talent." Maura paused before adding, "You owe Lord Silverwood your life, and yet you persist in harboring this long-held grudge against him."

Stacia allowed her head to drop back on the daybed. "No, I do not do that, my dear."

"I wish I had held my tongue when I suggested a way of revenge. Then matters might have become resolved by themselves."

"You are in no way to be held to blame, Maura. I have been seeking a means of retribution since I was eight years old."

She glanced at the manuscript of the play Mr. Allbury had left with her. "I daresay appearing in a comedy titled *The Fool* is entirely appropriate to my situation, and in any event I'm delighted to have something to do. I'm in a fidge to return to the stage as soon as I am able. It is the only life I have known or enjoyed since I was a child."

As Maura pushed one last long-stemmed rose into a vase, she pricked her finger on a thorn, and after she had sucked it thoughtfully for a moment

184

or two, she mused, "I cannot conceive why you don't consider throwing yourself on his lordship's mercy."

Stacia's answering laugh was a harsh one devoid of any mirth. "I recall Papa doing that to no avail. I doubt that he would be any more merciful with me."

"It's possible you might have misjudged him."

"No. I have been privileged to see him at his best as well as at his worst, and I tell you there is no possibility at all. Pride is everything to men like Blaise. He will not forgive a betrayal even if I could rid my memory of what he did," she answered in a forlorn voice as she began to read through the play, giving it her entire concentration.

Here, at least, was something she understood.

SIXTEEN

After taking tea with Maura, her friend decided to return to Tavistock Square in order to fetch some money for Stacia, who wished to tip vails to the servants who had cared for her so well during her stay at Lady Charlotte's house.

Not long after Maura had departed, a soft knock on her bedchamber door heralded the arrival of the earl, who entered the room hesitantly. Stacia's heart leaped at the sight of him, and then it was suffused with love, something that was both wonderful and alarming. Ultimately it would become more of a tragedy to her than her ruined childhood. This heartbreak, after all, would last a lifetime.

"Are you all alone?" he asked in a hushed tone as he stood in the doorway.

It was one of the few times she had witnessed him looking uncertain. "Maura has gone back home for a while, and I believe Lady Charlotte is dressing to go out for dinner."

"Then mayhap I should return later."

She couldn't help but smile at his strange sense of propriety. "Oh, do come in. Having once saved my life, you cannot exactly be made guilty of compromising me. In any event I am an actress, not a debutante."

He did come into the room but continued to appear uncomfortable about it. "This place is just like Covent Garden Market with all these flowers," he joked as he came further into the room. "I am told you are much improved, but if that is so, I cannot conceive why you remain closeted in this stuffy room alone when you could enjoy company downstairs."

"I shall be returning to my own home very soon now. It seemed unfair to impose upon the household any more than I already do."

"Your presence here is not regarded as an imposition. Lottie has found you delightful company. You must be aware of that."

Stacia looked away. "Her ladyship's kindness toward me has been unstinting, and you can be sure I have become exceedingly attached to her."

He'd brought a package in with him, and when he reached the daybed where she was sitting, he held it out to her. Looking up at him then, she asked, "What is it?"

"It is not, I promise you, more flowers. I would not, for anything, impose more of those upon you."

His ready wit always brought a smile to her lips, but as she reached out to take the parcel from him, her smile faded abruptly, for it was then that she noticed that his hands were bandaged.

"You're hurt!" she gasped. "Oh, my goodness! You were burned, too. Why did no one tell me?"

"I gave strict instructions you were not to be told. What use would it have been?" As he sat down beside her on the daybed, she touched his hands tentatively, and he assured her, "It's nothing. Just a slight scorch. I am able to tool the ribbons of the phaeton with no discomfort whatsoever."

187

"You would be able to drive to an inch whatever the injury, but I fear you are making little of it."

"I promise you it does not signify when compared to your own grievous injury."

At this point Stacia discovered she could not look into his face or bear his searching gaze for long, and she was forced to look away. Because she had always felt he could easily read her very soul, she harbored the fear now that he might somehow discern that sitting so close to him was a delightful torment to her. It took all her self-restraint for her to resist throwing herself into his arms, confessing her true identity, and begging to be held and loved by him for all time.

"Why don't you open the parcel?" he suggested, and she did then give her attention to the gift in the hope she would be diverted from her more shameful thoughts.

Her hands trembled slightly as she fumbled with the wrapping, which revealed a doll, dressed in a replica of the satin-and-lace gown she had worn as Dorabella, the anguished heroine of *The Devilish Earl*. The doll was so beautiful and the gift so thoughtful, tears came readily to her eyes once again.

"Do you like it?" he asked, and he sounded as eager as a child.

"It's the most beautiful gift I have ever received," she answered truthfully, and her voice was husky with emotion.

"I thought she would keep you company as you convalesce."

"She will always stay with me," Stacia vowed, hugging the doll close to her.

"I had something rather better than that in

mind," he told her, and his voice was as soft as a caress.

When she dared to raise her eyes to his again, there was a strange expression in them she could not recognize. Unconsciously she clutched the doll even closer to her as if it would protect her from her discomfiting thoughts.

"You saved my life," she whispered.

"Do you think I could have stayed there in the box and allowed you to burn even if you were playing Joan of Arc?"

She laughed nervously, touching his hands again. "I do trust you are being truthful with me. I couldn't bear to think you were hurt because of me."

"It's a mere bagatelle," he said, dismissing the matter with a small gesture of his hand. A moment later he became serious again. "I daresay I'd have leaped to your assistance even if I weren't madly in love with you."

When she looked at him again, she saw with no possible doubt he was being entirely genuine, and her eyes began to swim with tears, some of which spilled onto her cheeks.

He leaned forward and brushed them away with the tips of his bandaged fingers. "There, I'm a clumsy oaf to overset you. I hadn't meant for the conversation to turn serious. We'll speak at length when you've become stronger. I'll call in on the morrow, and in the meantime I shall leave you in the less-demanding company of little Dorabella."

For quite a long time after he had gone, she remained motionless, clutching the exquisite little doll to her heart, and then she flung herself down and sobbed into the cushion until she thought her heart would break.

Very early the following morning Stacia was awake and dressed, an easy feat to achieve as she had scarcely slept at all the previous night.

The irony wasn't lost on her that had she remained impervious to Lord Silverwood's charms, now would be the moment of her great triumph. Once he had confessed his love for her, revenge would have been hers to savor. Instead it produced an incredibly bitter taste.

As soon as she was able, she dispatched Maura on a few inessential errands that would occupy her for some considerable time, and then she waited until Lady Charlotte had departed to attend a fashionable breakfast before penning two brief notes, one of thanks to her ladyship and another of explanation to Maura. Having completed that task, she packed a few essential items in a cloak bag, including the doll, and went downstairs, where she bestowed generous vails on all the servants who had done her a service before entrusting the house steward with the delivery of the notes. Although he didn't question her when she asked him to hail a hackney carriage, he did look somewhat disdainful when entrusted with the task.

Emotion threatened to overcome her as the carriage moved away toward the Haymarket Inn, to which she had directed the jarvey to take her. There was no way of knowing when next she might see the earl, but whenever it was to be, they would have become strangers again. This time his emotions were involved, and his pride would not allow him to forgive her on a second occasion.

190

When she arrived at the inn, she discovered she would be obliged to endure a considerable wait before a chaise could be made available, however much she insisted upon the urgency of the matter. This *was* London, not some quiet rustic hostelry, she was told.

Fortunately on this, the second occasion she had run away, she possessed the means to bespeak a private parlor while she endured a wait that had become agonizing. For however long she was obliged to remain in London, she would be tormented by thoughts of how providence had robbed her yet again, but she was determined not to dwell on her loss lest she become bitter.

She had been bitter for years, she acknowledged at last, beyond anything that was necessary. Ironically it was Blaise Silverwood who had cured her of it, but in his doing so she had acquired an aching void where her heart ought to be.

By now her legs had begun to ache almost as much as her heart, and she supposed she shouldn't have been on them for as long as she had that day. Her eyelids began to droop, and she put her legs up on a stool and let her head drop back against the upholstered seat.

When a noise aroused her from her doze, Stacia had no notion how long she had drifted away into a light sleep, but when the door flew open, she fully expected to see the landlord standing there. Instead it was the earl who stood framed in the doorway, and Stacia sat up with a start.

"Wha . . . what are you doing here?" she stammered, her head reeling.

He looked uncompromisingly grim. "I assure you

I am not here to partake of the landlord's excellent hospitality."

"You're always funning," she protested tearfully. "I will not be pursued in this manner."

"You're more like to have your hide soundly thrashed, my girl. Don't you understand you're still too weak to be about on your own?"

"That's doing it too brown. I am quite bobbish, I thank you."

"You look as sick as a cushion," he responded, and then, throwing down his hat on a chair, he leveled his dark gaze at her as he slammed the door shut. "I believe it is time you stopped bamming me, Stacia. A stiff shot of honesty is long overdue."

She jumped to her feet, shocked to the core. "I have no notion what you may mean."

"Sit down," he ordered, and after hesitating for a moment, she was glad to do so, for her legs felt incredibly weak, and she hated to think he was correct in his assessment of her condition. "What makes you want to run away, Stacia? Away from an increasingly successful career and a man who loves you to distraction."

His confession was almost enough to overset her, and she was forced to turn her face away lest he suspect how much his presence affected her emotions. "I am not running away. I am merely traveling to recuperate at the coast."

"As I said, you must stop bamming me."

She couldn't meet his eyes, although she was beginning to find the gold tassels on his Hessian boots fascinating as they quivered with every move he made.

"How did you contrive to find me?" she asked.

"With surprising ease, you silly goose. You can't

escape me so easily. I prevailed upon Mrs. Copeland to reveal to me the contents of your note. She was most obliging, unlike you, I might add."

Stacia choked back a gasp of annoyance. "How could she do such a thing?"

"Out of a genuine concern for your well-being, I imagine."

Tears of frustration and anger stung her eyes. "I entreated her not to reveal the contents of the note to anyone."

"I don't believe she considered the order included me. In any event even if Mrs. Copeland hadn't possessed the good sense to tell me, my sister's servants are bound to have overheard your direction to the jarvey, and they are always obliging." She drew a profound sigh as he asked, "Why on earth are you going to Brighton, of all places?"

She bridled indignantly. "Why should I not go to Brighton, pray?"

"Because it has become passé."

"I don't give a fiddlestick whether it is fashionable or not," she declared. "My very good friends Mr. and Mrs. Ormerod Greaves are resident there, and they wrote to invite me to convalesce with them. The sea air, they believe, will be beneficial to me." He appeared disbelieving, and she added, "When I return, I am to marry Mr. Kingswell."

"Paris Kingswell, that man-milliner! Oh, no, you are not going to marry him!"

"It has nothing to do with you."

"It has everything to do with me. You cannot marry us both, and I intend you to be *my* wife."

Stacia recoiled with shock. "Blaise! You cannot know what you're saying."

"A real possibility, and it is entirely like my at-

193

tic's to let in wishing to become leg-shackled to you, especially if spinning cuffers is a lifelong habit of yours, but be certain I do mean it."

"I'm an actress."

"It's impossible not to be aware of that fact," he answered, and for the first time she detected his mood softening.

"Then you must also be aware of why I cannot possibly marry you, or rather the reason you should not marry me."

"Are you already buckled to another? A youthful marriage conveniently forgotten?"

"No!"

"Then you will marry me and soon. Let there be no more argument. I know you love me, so you can't bam me on that score."

"Titled gentlemen do not marry actresses," she pointed out, her voice now touched with poignancy.

"I know of several who have done so and lived happily to recommend it. If you insist upon making dainty, my love, I shall instead become riveted to Miss Eustacia Farramond of Dover's End. Will that suit your sense of propriety better?"

Stacia clapped one hand to her lips. "My stars! How did you know?"

"Do you consider me a gull-catcher? I've long since cut my eyeteeth, so I was bound to find out eventually."

Her eyes narrowed then. "Did you know me in Dorrington?"

"Not as early as that, I confess. How could I? I was merely taken by your beauty and talent on that occasion. I confess to you now, Stacia, no female had ever rebuffed me quite so cruelly as you. I was mortified, you may be sure. If I'd known then you were Eustacia Farramond, I might have been more understanding of your attitude."

"You might equally have informed my uncle Quentin of my whereabouts."

"That, I assure you, would have gone entirely against the pluck. More like I would have planted him a facer for his ill-usage of you."

Stacia almost laughed out loud at the image he conjured up in her mind, but a moment later she hardly dared to ask, "Just how long *have* you known?"

"Long enough," he replied with a smugness that irritated her.

"Was . . . was it before we rode for the first time in Hyde Park?"

"Not quite as early as that, but reasonably soon afterward." Stacia gave out a small cry of dismay as he went on. "It was Hu who raised my initial suspicion on the night of Lottie's soiree. He saw you in an intimate coze with Damian Farramond and jumped—no, leaped—to the conclusion you were sweet upon each other."

Now Stacia definitely couldn't stop herself from chuckling, and the earl said wryly, "Exactly my feelings. I knew the fellow wasn't in the petticoat line, and then I recalled there were certain similarities between you, for those who looked close enough."

"Oh, surely not."

"Not very great, I own," he hastened to assure her, "but sufficient to make me curious, for I recalled he did have a sister." Stacia grew tense once more at the merest reference to that awful night. "So I made bold and asked him about her—you, as

195

it turned out. He told me his sister had died as a child."

"The muckworm!"

"His answer didn't endear him to me, I promise you. To cut line, Stacia, I did press him most forcefully, and eventually he confessed the truth to me."

"It must have been wrought out of him."

"He'll come about most handsomely once you're Lady Silverwood."

She shivered delightedly at the notion as he went on, "He merely confirmed what I had already come to suspect."

"You are very astute, my lord."

"Only because you were constantly on my mind." Her eyes met his meltingly, and he added, "If you weren't so highly born, that wager wouldn't have made you fly up into the boughs as it did. All the actresses of my acquaintance would regard it as an honor and be in high snuff."

"All the actresses of your acquaintance . . ." she gasped, feeling outraged anew, and he held up his hands in mock surrender.

"You are the last, I assure you."

"As you are a man of honor, I trust your word, but why on earth did you allow me to continue the pretense once you knew my true identity?"

"An actress is entitled to adopt a stage name, is she not? There is nothing unusual in that, although you'd known who *I* was from the outset and yet you didn't speak of it to me." Her head drooped, and she was relieved when he added, "It came as a great relief to me to know why you had taken me in dislike."

"Is it impossible for someone not to respond favorably to your charm?"

"It is unusual."

Stacia bit back a gasp of annoyance. "You are so puffed-up," she accused.

"You will be obliged to accept that in me."

"As long as you do not demand the impossible of me."

"It's a bargain." They stood smiling at each other for a long moment before his brow furrowed slightly and he asked, "Stacia, what had you planned for me in this little drama of yours?" Her face grew stiff, and when she didn't answer, he suggested, with a wicked gleam in his eye, "I suspect you hoped to make a May game of me. You wanted to make me love you so you could reject me. Was that to be your revenge, my little schemer?"

Once again her head dropped. "Some revenge, when I fell in love with you beyond all reason."

He rested the back of his hand against her damp cheek. "You were such a beautiful child. The memory of you and that night haunted me for years. Mayhap that is what drew me to you when I saw you again—that dim, distant memory of a child bewildered and afraid for her future."

"I hated you for so long, but it wasn't hard to adjust to loving you. It came so easily to me." She raised her head to look at him again. "I have never been able to comprehend why you repossessed Dover's End, Blaise. You had no need of it, and it was all we had left."

"I had no choice," he answered in an abrupt tone, drawing back from her a little. "I assure you it was the most difficult thing I have ever had to do in my entire life."

"Don't seek to gammon me. You owned the house by default. You could have let us live in it. Surely

197

you didn't need to destroy what little we had left in life."

"I told you, Stacia, I really and truly had no choice in the matter. The supreme irony of the situation is that you've been hating the wrong man for all these years. I was just there as a messenger on behalf of my uncle, who was ill at the time with the gout. *He* was Lord Silverwood at the time, before he drank himself into an early grave. My father briefly inherited the title, and then it came to me."

Stunned, Stacia could only ask, "What happened to the house?"

"I have no notion, but I surmise my uncle sold it immediately to raise funds to fend off the duns. Your father was not the only one who was feckless. My uncle was totally in debt. Apart from the title there was nothing to inherit after his death. Quite a facer for you, I imagine."

"A thunderbolt, more like," she confessed. Then she glanced at him curiously. "You've known for an age why I took you in dislike, yet you didn't tell me all this. Why?"

He shrugged. "It was a May game for both of us, until you nearly cooked yourself and I understood at last when you were almost lost to me that the playacting had to end. There was no room for humdudgeon if love was to thrive." Stacia smiled faintly at the wisdom of his words, and then he went on, giving her a beseeching look, "You needn't imagine I am as much of a scapegrace as my late, unlamented uncle. His behavior was an abject lesson to me, you may be sure. I don't gamble deep. I have no wish to game away my possessions, nor own anyone else's."

198

"Blaise, I am so sorry. I didn't mean to put the bridle on the wrong horse."

"You're not to be held responsible, and I believe enough time has been spent on regrets. It's time for us to look to the future. No more running away, Stacia. Twice is outside of enough."

She blushed as she reminded him, "You once boasted to me that retaining your bachelor status was of the greatest import to you."

"I confess that it was once, but no more. You are the most important matter on my mind and in my life. You have been for quite some time now," he went on with hardly a pause, drawing her to her feet and close to him. "I can't offer you Dover's End, but I can promise you a home of your own, and you'll never be in want again."

Trembling slightly with emotion, Stacia slid her arms around his neck and looked up at him. "You are all I shall ever want, my own sweet love," she whispered, before offering her face up for his kiss.